'Kjære' Isabel 'og Miriam.
Here are some tr☑ [P9-CIV-871] wegian
fairy tales...I hope you enjoy them.
Lots of love,
Miss 'tante' Gaye

NORWEGIAN
FOLK TALES

NORWEGIAN FOLK TALES

From the collection of
PETER CHRISTEN ASBJØRNSEN
JØRGEN MOE

Illustrated by
ERIK WERENSKIOLD
THEODOR KITTELSEN

Translated by
PAT SHAW
CARL NORMAN

PANTHEON BOOKS, NEW YORK

Published in the United States by Pantheon Books, a division of Random House, Inc., New York, and simultaneously in Canada by Random House of Canada Limited, Toronto. Originally published in Norway by Dreyers Forlag.

Library of Congress Cataloging in Publication Data

Asbjørnsen, Peter Christen, 1812–1885.
Norwegian folk tales.

Translation of: Norske folke-eventyr.
Reprint. Originally published: Oslo : Dreyers
Forlag, 1960.
1. Fairy tales—Norway.   I. Moe, Jørgen
Engebretsen, 1813–1882.   II. Iversen, Pat Shaw.
III. Norman, Carl.   IV. Title.
PT8661.A8   1982   398.2′109481   82-6401
ISBN 0-394-71054-1   AACR2

Manufactured in the United States of America
8 C 9 7

CONTENTS

THE NORWEGIAN FOLK TALES
AND THEIR ILLUSTRATORS

Pat Shaw

If Norway were to show the world a single work of art which would most truly express the Norwegian character, perhaps the best choice would be the folk tales, published for the first time more than a hundred years ago and later illustrated by Erik Werenskiold and Theodor Kittelsen.

The folk tales of countries in more southern latitudes have preserved more of the romantic splendor that characterizes the folk tales which originated in the Far East and thence spread throughout the world. The Norwegian folk tales, however, contain an undertone of realism and folk humor that makes them unique. The Grimm brothers, collectors of some of the most famous folk tale classics, were aware of this. The Norwegian folk tales, said Jacob Grimm, have a freshness and a fullness that "surpass nearly all others".

The tales, or *eventyr* as they are called, wandered to Norway probably during the Middle Ages. They were absorbed into the existing lore, undergoing constant change through generations of storytelling. The storytellers themselves were highly esteemed if they were good, and each one had his own style of telling a story. It seems that there was a difference between the stories told by old men and old women. The old women usually kept to deep, mystic or eerie themes, while the men best related humorous, sometimes bawdy, stories.

Rural life in Norway has always been centered in the family farms — small isolated communities, often surrounded by great forests and high mountains. There, according to Werenskiold's description of his childhood home, "one sat in the darkness by the oven door ... from the time of the tallow candle and the rush light ... in the endless, lonely winter evenings, where folk still saw the *nisse* and captured the sea-serpent, and swore that it was true." In the old days the Church was the sole authority in life and faith, but everyday problems were solved by *belief* — belief that was never questioned.

The folk tales reflect the tremendous imagination of the people as well as their independence and self-reliance. A Norse historian once complained that the tales always "belittle the king". He referred to the fact that the king was

5

often depicted as a fat, genial farmer who could be approached as an equal. There is biting satire in the tales, and the humor is often broad and earthy. The representatives of the Church are treated rather irreverently. Nonetheless, standards of guilt and justice prevail, and moral law is present, even in the world of the Trolls. The Trolls are awesome, but stupid, and are invariably outwitted and vanquished. The hero is *Askeladden* (literally, the Ash Lad, because he always sits by the fire and roots and pokes in the ashes). He is the youngest, the dreamer, the "ne'er-do-well", often despised by his parents and brothers. However, he is kind and honest, and possesses an open, unprejudiced mind. Of humble birth, he surmounts overwhelming obstacles to win the princess and half the kingdom.

Near the middle of the nineteenth century scholars began "discovering" a rich, native tradition that had lain fallow and almost forgotten during the years of foreign cultural influence. Ballads, painting and folk music were unearthed and revived in the "National Renaissance" that was sweeping through the greater part of Europe at that time. Among the Norwegian scholars of native culture were the two men responsible for the most extensive collection of Norwegian folk tales ever made — Peter Christen Asbjørnsen and Jørgen Moe.

Peter Christen Asbjørnsen was born in 1812, in Christiania (now Oslo), where his father was a glazier. In his childhood he heard *eventyr* from the workmen and apprentices in his father's workshop. These apprentices, who came from all parts of the country, often took Asbjørnsen along on their Sunday excursions while he was still very young, and, according to one of his friends, "thereby instilled in him a growing interest in the life of forest and field". In 1824 his father sent him to a school in Norderhov, north of Christiania. The two-year stay, in a rural community steeped in traditions, made a deep impression on him. But of the greatest importance was his meeting with Jørgen Moe, who was to become his closest friend and later his collaborator in writing down the folk tales.

Jørgen Moe was born on a farm at Hole in Ringerike. Jørgen evidenced his love for books at an early age and became a voracious reader. Asbjørnsen and Moe met at the Norderhov School in the summer of 1826. The two boys had many interests in common, especially their love for the outdoors. They spent every spare hour together hunting, fishing, or taking long hikes, and both dreamt of the day when they would be poets.

In 1834, Asbjørnsen went to Romerike in eastern Norway, where he remained for three years as a private tutor. During his student days he had begun writing down some of the folk tales he had heard in his childhood, and later in Norderhov. Once more surrounded by the living tradition, he kept up his avocation.

The first collection of Norwegian folklore, published in 1833, by a clergyman, Andreas Faye, aroused considerable public interest. Two years later, when it was rumored that Faye contemplated another collection, an assistant in the State Archives sent him some stories that had not appeared in his first book, including three "from one of my friends, student Asbjørnsen". Faye was most appreciative, and sent Asbjørnsen a letter of thanks in which he concluded by saying, "I hereby appoint you Folk-Lore-Ambassador-Extraordinary." Accepting this challenge, Asbjørnsen soon submitted twelve legends and a folk song.

At this time he began thinking seriously of publishing a folk tale collection of his own, and discussed with Jorgen Moe the possibility of collaborating on such a project. They did not come to a serious agreement, however, until they had both read Grimm's *Kinder und Hausmärchen*. In a joint letter to Jacob Grimm, written in 1844, they describe how "an early acquaintanceship with your honorable *Kinder- und Hausmärchen*, and an intimate knowledge of the lore and life of the people in our homeland, gave us the idea, eight years ago, of preparing a collection of Norwegian folk tales."

The first volume of *Norwegian Folk Tales*, collected by Peter Christen Asbjørnsen and Jørgen Moe, appeared in 1845. After the second edition in 1852, the book became exceedingly popular. The collaborators continued their research, one covering Gudbrandsdal and the other Telemark, districts rich in folk tradition. As the result of these and other trips, they published additional volumes as well as single stories in newspapers and magazines. However, as Jørgen Moe's clerical duties took up more and more of his time, he was gradually forced to abandon active collecting and research. His son, Moltke, had acquired an interest in the folk tradition at an early age, and it was not long before he had stepped into his father's shoes, and was collaborating with Asbjørnsen. He later became an distinguished folklorist in his own right, and his contributions to the Norwegian folk tradition are manifold.

For some time Asbjørnsen had contemplated an illustrated edition of the folk tales. This project was not realized, however, until 1879. Some of the most famous Norwegian painters of the time were selected to do the drawings, along with a young, unknown artist, Erik Werenskiold.

Erik Werenskiold was born in 1855, in Kongsvinger where his father was commander of the town fortress. Even in his childhood Werenskiold was a keen observer of nature and people, and his father told him folk tales and read aloud from the ancient myths and sagas. At the age of seventeen Werenskiold entered the University, but after a year he decided that he was more interested in studying art. In 1874, he enrolled at the Royal Norwegian Art School — much against his father's wishes. At that time Munich was a mecca for Norwegian art students. Werenskiold arrived there in 1875, and remained for five years.

His first drawing for the folk tales was composed to illustrate the tale"Taper-Tom Who Made the King's Daughter Laugh". In the summer of 1877, when plans were under way for the illustrated edition, this and others of his drawings were shown to Asbjørnsen. Delighted with Werenskiold's work, Asbjørnsen invited him to participate in the project.

Realizing that he had seen very little of Norway, Werenskiold went to Vågå and Lom, in the Gudbrandsdal valley, to familiarize himself with the setting of the folk tales. On the large old farms he found the ancient patriarchal customs still alive. As he once remarked, "Here on the great farms there were still small kings, and the tenant farmers were their serfs. Behind this primitive life, behind these vigorous, strongly pronounced human types, and this unique architecture, one could sense the Middle Ages; and behind the large forest lay the Troll world of the Jotunheim mountains. I have never since found anything that seemed more Norwegian to me than Vågå!"

In Werenskiold's drawings, the king appears as the farmers must have imagined him. He wears crown and scepter, and generally shuffles around in slippers, smoking a long pipe. Genial in appearance, he is also gruff and authoritative. Werenskiold brings the *eventyr* world to life by using the valleys and forests and rural architecture of eastern Norway as a natural setting.

The drawings for the folk tales established Werenskiold as one of Norway's foremost artists. Asbjørnsen realized that he had found the right man, and, when the second illustrated edition was planned, Werenskiold alone of the original group was asked to carry on. He immediately requested that one of his friends, a completely unknown artist named Theodor Kittelsen, be invited to work with him.

Theodor Kittelsen was born in Kragerø in 1857. He started to draw at a very tender age, and was considered by his townspeople as somewhat of a prodigy. Having attended an art school in Christiania for about two years, he continued his studies in Munich, where he arrived in 1876, and where he met Werenskiold.

Werenskiold seemed to have sensed that Kittelsen's temperament was even closer to the folk tales than his own. In a letter to Asbjørnsen, Werenskiold wrote, "Kittelsen has a wild, individual, inventive fantasy . . . . For many years I have had the constant thought that he should be the man to do that side of your *eventyr* which none of the rest of us has yet been able to accomplish, namely the purely fantastic creations!"

At first, Asbjørnsen was shocked by the power and originality of these drawings, which bore no resemblance to the pale romanticism of contemporary art. When trying them out on children, however, he realized that they satisfied the unspoiled juvenile hunger for fantasy. Thus, Kittelsen was brought in on the project in 1881, and the happy collaboration began.

The tales, as illustrated by Werenskiold and Kittelsen, quickly established themselves as a national treasure. There is no doubt that they have had a considerable impact upon Norway's cultural history, and they are cherished and read with as much enthusiasm today as when they were first published.

THE BOYS WHO MET THE TROLLS
IN THE HEDAL WOODS

On a small farm in Vågå, in Gudbrandsdal, there once lived, in the old days, a poor couple. They had many children, and two of the sons, who were half-grown, always had to wander about the countryside begging. So they were familiar with all the roads and trails, and they also knew the short cut to Hedal.

One day they wanted to go there, but they had heard that some falconers had built a hut at Mæla, and they wanted to stop there too, to see the birds and how the men caught them, so they took the footpath over Longmoss. But it was already late in the fall and the dairymaids had gone home from the summer pastures, and there was nowhere the boys could find shelter, nor food either. So they had to keep to the road to Hedal, but that was only an overgrown cowpath, and when darkness came they lost the path, nor did they find the falconers' hut either, and before they knew it, they were right in the midst of the thickest part of the Bjølstad forest. When they realized that they couldn't find their way out, they started cutting branches, made up a fire, and built themselves a shelter of pine branches, for they had a hatchet with them. And then they gathered heather and moss, of which they made a bed.

A while after they had lain down, they heard something snuffing and snorting very hard. The boys were all ears, and listened well to hear whether it might

Drawings by Erik Werenskiold

be an animal or a Forest Troll which they heard. But then it started snorting even harder and said, "I smell the smell of Christian blood here!"

Then they heard it tread so heavily that the earth shook under it, and they could tell that the Trolls were out.

"God help us! What'll we do now?" said the younger boy to his brother.

"Oh, you'll just have to stay under the fir tree where you're standing, and be ready to take the bags and run for your life when you see them coming! I'll take the hatchet," said the other.

Just then they saw the Trolls come rushing, and they were so big and tall that their heads were level with the tops of the fir trees. But they had only one eye among the three of them, and they took turns using it. Each had a hole in his forehead to put it in, and guided it with his hands. The one who went ahead had to have it, and the others went behind him and held onto him.

"Take to your heels!" said the elder of the boys. "But don't run too far before you see how it goes. Since they have the eye so high up, it'll be hard for them to see me when I come behind them."

Well, the brother ran ahead, with the Trolls at his heels. In the meantime, the elder brother went behind them and chopped the hindmost Troll in the ankle, so that he let out a horrible shriek. Then the first Troll became so frightened that he jumped, and dropped the eye, and the boy wasn't slow in grabbing it up. It was bigger than two pot lids put together, and it was so clear, that even though it was pitch black, the night became as light as day when he looked through it.

When the Trolls discovered that he had taken the eye from them, and that he had wounded one of them, they started threatening him with all the evil there was, if he didn't give them back the eye that very minute.

"I'm not afraid of Trolls or threats," said the boy. "Now I have three eyes to myself, and you don't have any. And still two of you have to carry the third."

"If we don't get our eye back this very minute, you'll be turned into sticks and stones!" shrieked the Trolls.

But the boy felt there wasn't any hurry; he was afraid of neither boasting nor magic, he said. If they didn't leave him alone, he would chop at all three of them so they would have to crawl along the hill like creeping, crawling worms.

When the Trolls heard this, they became frightened and started to sing another tune. They pleaded quite nicely that, if he gave them back the eye, he would get both gold and silver, and everything he wanted. Well, the boy thought that was all very fine, but he wanted the gold and silver first. So he said that if one of them would go home and fetch so much gold and silver that he and his brother could fill their bags, and give him and his brother two good steel bows besides, they should get the eye. But until then he would keep it.

The Trolls carried on and said that none of them could walk as long as he didn't have an eye to see with. But then one of them started yelling for the old woman, for they had *one* old woman among the three of them. After a while there was an answer in a mountain far to the north. So the Trolls said that she

10

The Trolls had only one eye among them, and they took turns using it.

The boys come home.

was to come with two steel bows, and two pails full of gold and silver, and it
wasn't long before she was there. When she saw what had happened, she
started threatening with magic. But the Trolls became still more frightened and
bade her be careful of that little wasp. She couldn't be certain that he wouldn't
take her eye, too. So she flung the buckets, and the gold and the silver, and the
bows at them, and strode home to the mountain with the Trolls. And since
then, no one has ever heard that the Trolls have been about in the Hedal Woods
sniffing after Christian blood.

THE SEVENTH FATHER
OF THE HOUSE

There was once a man who was travelling. He came, at last, to a beautiful, big farm. It had a manor house so fine that it could easily have been a small castle.

"This will be a good place to rest," he said to himself as he went in through the gate. An old man, with grey hair and beard, was chopping wood nearby.

"Good evening, father," said the traveller. "Can you put me up for the night?"

"I'm not the father of the house," said the old one. "Go into the kitchen and talk to my father."

The traveller went into the kitchen. There he found a man who was even older, down on his knees in front of the hearth, blowing on the fire.

"Good evening, father. Can you put me up for the night?" said the traveller.

"I'm not the father of the house," said the old fellow. "But go in and talk to my father. He's sitting by the table in the parlor."

So the traveller went into the parlor and talked to the man who was sitting

Drawings by Erik Werenskiold

by the table. He was much older than both the others, and he sat, shivering and shaking, his teeth chattering, reading from a big book almost like a little child.

"Good evening, father. Will you put me up for the night?" said the man.

"I'm not the father of the house, but talk to my father who's sitting on the settle," said the old man who sat by the table, shivering and shaking, his teeth chattering.

So the traveller went over to the one who was sitting on the settle, and he was busy trying to smoke a pipe of tobacco. But he was so huddled up, and his hands shook so that he could hardly hold onto the pipe.

"Good evening, father," said the traveller again. "Can you put me up for the night?"

"I'm not the father of the house," replied the huddled up old fellow. "But talk to my father who's lying in the bed."

The traveller went over to the bed, and there lay an old, old man in whom there was no sign of life but a pair of big eyes.

"Good evening, father. Can you put me up for the night?" said the traveller.

"I'm not the father of the house, but talk to my father who's lying in the cradle," said the man with the big eyes.

Well, the traveller went over to the cradle. There lay an ancient fellow, so shrivelled up that he was no bigger than a baby. And there was no way of telling there was life in him except for a rattle in his throat now and then.

"Good evening, father. Can you put me up for the night?" said the man.

It took a long time before he got an answer, and even longer before the fellow finished it. He said — he like all the others — that he was not the father of the house. "But talk to my father. He's hanging in the horn on the wall."

The traveller stared up along the walls, and at last he caught sight of the horn, too. But when he tried to see the one who was lying in it, there was nothing

to be seen but a little ash-white form that had the likeness of a human face.

Then he was so frightened that he cried aloud: "GOOD EVENING, FATHER! WILL YOU PUT ME UP FOR THE NIGHT?"

There was a squeaking sound up in the horn like a tiny titmouse, and it was all he could do to make out that the sound meant: "Yes, my child."

Then in came a table decked with the costliest dishes, and with ale and spirits, too. And when the traveller had eaten and drunk, in came a good bed covered with reindeer hides. And he was very glad that at last he had found the true father of the house.

THE PARSON AND THE SEXTON

There was once a parson who was such a blusterer that whenever he saw anyone come driving towards him on the highway, he would roar from afar: *"Off the road! Off the road! Here comes the parson himself!"*

Once when he was carrying on like this, he met the king.

"Off the road! Off the road!" he shouted a long way off; but the king kept on driving straight ahead. So, for once, the parson had to turn his horse aside. And when the king came alongside he said, "Tomorrow you shall come to the court. And if you can't answer three questions I am going to put to you, you shall lose both frock and collar for the sake of your pride!"

This was quite a different tune from what the parson was used to. Bluster and bellow he could, and carry on worse than bad, too. But question-and-answer was out of his field. So he went to the sexton, who was said to have a better head on his shoulders than the parson, and told him that *he* wasn't keen on going, "for one fool can ask more than ten wise men can answer," he said. And so he got the sexton to go in his place.

Well, the sexton went; and he came to the royal manor dressed in the parson's frock and ruff collar. The king met him out on the porch, wearing both crown and scepter, and looking so grand he fairly shone.

"So you're there, are you?" said the king.

Yes he was .... that was sure enough.

"Now, tell me first," said the king, "how far is it from east to west?"

"That's a day's journey, that is," said the sexton.

"How so?" asked the king.

"We....ll, the sun rises in the east and sets in the west, and does it nicely in a day," said the sexton.

Drawings by Erik Werenskiold

"Tell me what I'm thinking now!"

"All right," said the king, "but tell me now, what do you think I'm worth, just as you see me here?"

"Let's see, Christ was valued at thirty pieces of silver, so I'd better not set you any higher than....twenty-nine," said the sexton.

"Mmmmmmmmmmmmm!" said the king. "Well, since you're so wise on all counts, tell me what I'm thinking now!"

"Oh, I suppose you're thinking that it's the parson who's standing here before you. But I'm sorry to say you're wrong, for it's the sexton!"

"Aha! Then go home with you, and *you* be parson and let *him* be sexton!" said the king.

And so it was!

THE ASH LAD WHO MADE THE PRINCESS SAY,
"YOU'RE A LIAR!"

There was once a king who had a daughter, and she was such a liar that no one could equal her. So he made it known that the one who could lie so that he made her say, "You're a liar!" would get both her and half the kingdom. There were many who tried, for everyone was only too willing to have the princess and half the kingdom, but all of them fared badly.

Then there were three brothers who were bent upon trying their luck. The two eldest set out first, but they fared no better than all the others. So the Ash Lad set out, and he met the princess in the stable.

"Good day!" he said. "It's a pleasure to meet you."

"Good day," she said. "It's nice to meet you, too! You don't have as big a barn as we do," she said, "for, when a shepherd stands at each end and blows on a ram's horn, one can't hear the other!"

"Oh, yes indeed!" said the boy. "Ours is much bigger, for when a cow is got with calf at one end of it, she doesn't bear it before she gets to the other."

"You don't say so!" said the princess. "Well, you haven't such a big ox as we do. There you can see it! When a man sits on each horn, one can't reach the other with a twelve-foot pole!"

Drawings by Erik Werenskiold

"We have an ox so big that, when someone is sitting on each horn
blowing a lure, one can't hear the other!"

"Pooh!" said the boy. "We have an ox so big that, when someone is sitting on each horn blowing a lure, one can't hear the other!"

"Oh indeed?" said the princess. "But you don't have as much milk as we do, all the same," she said, "for we milk into enormous troughs, and carry it in and pour it into big cauldrons, and curdle big cheeses!"

"Oh, we milk into great cauldrons, and cart them in and pour it into huge brewing vats, and curdle cheeses as big as a house. And then we have a grey mare to tread the cheese. But once it foaled in the cheese, and after we had been eating cheese for seven years, we came upon a big grey horse. I was going to drive to the mill with it one day, then its backbone broke; but I knew a remedy for that. I took a spruce tree and put it in for a backbone, and no other back did the horse have as long as we had it. But that tree grew, and became so big that I climbed up to Heaven through it, and when I got there, one of the saints was sitting weaving a bristle rope of barley broth. All at once the spruce broke and I couldn't get down again, but the good saint lowered me down on one of the ropes, and I landed in a fox's den. And there sat my mother and your father patching shoes, and all at once my mother gave your father such a blow that the scurf flew off 'im!"

"You're a liar!" said the princess. "My father's never been scurvy in his life!"

TAPER-TOM WHO MADE THE PRINCESS LAUGH

There was once a king who had a daughter, and she was so beautiful that she was known both far and wide; but she took herself so seriously that she could never laugh, and then she was so haughty that she said "No" to everyone who came and courted her. She would not have anyone, no matter how fine, whether he was prince or gentleman. The king had long since tired of this, and felt that she could get married like the others; she had nothing to wait for, she was old enough; nor would she be any richer, either, for she was to have half the kingdom, which she inherited from her mother.

So the king had it proclaimed from all the pulpits in the land, both quickly and soon, that the one who could make his daughter laugh was to get her and half the kingdom. But if anyone tried and failed, he was to have three strips cut out of his back and salt rubbed in. And it's certain that there were many sore backs in *that* kingdom. Suitors came from south and from north, and from east and from west, and believed it would be an easy matter to make the king's daughter laugh. And queer fellows came too. But for all the monkeys there were, and for all the monkeyshines they did, the king's daughter was just as gloomy and serious as ever.

Drawings by Erik Werenskiold

Close to the king's manor there lived a man who had three sons. They also heard that the king had proclaimed that the one who could make the king's daughter laugh was to get her and half the kingdom.

The eldest wanted to set out first; so he rushed off, and when he came to the king's manor, he told the king that he wanted to try to make the princess laugh.

"Well, to be sure," said the king, "but it will be of little use, my man, for there have been many here who have tried. My daughter is so serious that it is no use, and I don't like to see more get into trouble."

But the boy felt it would be of some use. It couldn't be so much trouble to make a king's daughter laugh for *him*, for both highborn and lowborn had laughed at him so many times when he had served as a soldier and drilled under Nils sergeant. So he started marching up and down outside the princess' window, doing all the mistakes he used to do as a recruit. But it didn't help. The king's daughter was just as gloomy and serious. So they took him and cut three broad strips out of his back, and sent him home again.

When he had come safely home, the second son wanted to set out. He was a schoolmaster, and a strange figure of a man he was, too. He had legs of unequal length, and that with a vengeance. One minute he was as short as a boy, then he stood up on his long leg and became as tall as a Troll. And he was really a champion at running.

Yes, he too set out for the king's manor and said he wanted to try to make the king's daughter laugh. That wasn't at all unlikely, thought the king, "but heaven help you if you don't!" he said. "We cut the strips broader for each one who tries!"

The schoolmaster strode out on the field. There he placed himself outside the princess' window, and he preached and said Mass like seven parsons, and read and sang like seven sextons who had been in the parish there. The king laughed so that he had to hold onto the porch post, and the king's daughter almost cracked a smile, but she caught herself and was just as gloomy and serious again, and so it went no better with Paul the Schoolmaster than it had gone with Per the Soldier — for they were called Per and Paul, you might know. They took him, and cut three strips out of his back, and rubbed in salt, and then they sent him home again.

Then the youngest wanted to set out, and that one was Taper-Tom. But the brothers laughed and made fun of him, and showed him their sore backs; and the father wouldn't let him go, for he said it couldn't be of any use for *him* who had no sense. He knew nothing and did nothing, but only sat by the hearth like a cat and poked in the ashes and whittled pine torches. But Taper-Tom didn't give in. He nagged and whined so long that they grew tired of it, and at last he was allowed to go to the king's manor and try his luck.

When he came to the king's court, he didn't say that he wanted to make the king's daughter laugh, but asked if he could get a serving-job there. No, they had no serving-job for him, but Taper-Tom didn't give up. They certainly could

21

make use of one who could carry wood and water to the kitchen maids on such a big farm, he said. Well, the king didn't think that could be so unlikely, and he was pretty well tired of Taper-Tom's whining, he too; and at last Taper-Tom was allowed to stay there, and carry wood and water to the kitchen maids.

One day, as he was fetching water from the brook, he caught sight of a big fish lurking under an old fir root, where the water had washed the earth away. He put his bucket carefully under the fish and caught it. But on the way back to the king's manor, he met an old crone who was leading a golden goose.

"Good day, grandmother!" said Taper-Tom. "That's a fine bird you have; and such splendid feathers, now! They shine a long way off — if one had such feathers, there'd be no need to whittle pine torches," he said.

The old woman thought just as well of the fish Taper-Tom had in his bucket. So she said that if he would give her the fish, he could have the golden goose. And the goose was such that if any person so much as touched it, he would be stuck fast if Taper-Tom just said, "Hang on, if you want to come along!"

Well, Taper-Tom was quite willing to swap. "A bird is just as good as a fish," he said to himself. "And, if it's the way you say, I can easily use it as a fishhook," he said to the old crone, and was well pleased with the goose.

He hadn't gone very far before he met an old woman. When she saw that fine golden goose, she just had to come over and touch it. So she made herself nice and sweet, and then she asked Taper-Tom if she couldn't pet his pretty golden goose.

"All right," said Taper-Tom, "but you mustn't take any of her feathers." The very moment she put her hand on the goose, he said, "Hang on, if you want to come along!" The old woman pulled and tugged, but she had to hang on, whether she wanted to or not, and Taper-Tom walked on as if he were alone with the golden goose.

When he had travelled a little farther, he met a man who had a score to settle with the old woman for a trick she had played on him; and when he saw her struggling so hard to get loose, and understood that she was stuck fast, he thought he could safely give her a blow, and so he gave her a swift kick with one foot.

"Hang on, if you want to come along!" cried Taper-Tom, and the man had to follow along and hop on one foot, whether he wanted to or not. When he pulled and struggled and wanted to get loose, it was even worse, for then he nearly fell over backwards.

Now they trudged along for a good while until they were close to the king's manor. There they met the king's blacksmith. He was on his way to the smithy and had a big pair of tongs in his hand. This smith was a jester, who was always full of fun and rascally tricks, and when he saw this procession come hopping and hobbling along, he almost doubled up with laughter. But then he said, "This must be a flock of geese for the princess. Now who's gander and who's goose? That must be the gander, the one who's jogging along in front. Goosie! Goosie!

And so with his tongs he grabbed the old man by the seat of the breeches.

Goosie! Goosie! Goosie!" he called, and threw out his hand as if he were scattering corn to the geese.

But the procession did not stop — the old woman and the man just glared at the smith for making fun of them.

So the smith said, "It would be fun to hold back the whole flock of geese, as many as they are." For he was a strong man. And so with his tongs he grabbed the old man by the seat of his breeches, and the old fellow began to shout and wriggle.

But Taper-Tom said, "Hang on, if you want to come along!"

So the smith also had to go along. And for all he bent his back, and dug his heels in the ground and wanted to get loose, it helped not one bit. He was stuck as fast as though he had been screwed into the big anvil in the smithy, and whether he wanted to or not, he had to dance along.

When they arrived at the king's manor, the watchdog flew at them and started barking as if they were tramps or thieves, and when the king's daughter looked out of the window to see what was going on, and caught sight of this gang of scarecrows, she burst out laughing. But Taper-Tom wasn't satisfied with that.

"Wait a moment, and she'll soon be splitting her sides!" he said, and turned back of the king's manor with his procession.

As they came past the kitchen, the door stood open and the cook was busy stirring the porridge. But when she caught sight of Taper-Tom and his flock, she rushed out of the kitchen, with the ladle in one hand and the pot of steaming porridge in the other, and laughed until she shook. And when she saw that the smith was along, she slapped her thighs and screamed with laughter. But when

23

she had really laughed her fill, *she* also thought that the golden goose was so fine that she had to go over and stroke it.

"Taper-Tom, Taper-Tom," she cried, running after him with the porridge ladle in her hand. "May I stroke that lovely bird you have?"

"Let her stroke me instead!" said the smith.

"So I will!" said Taper-Tom.

But when the cook heard that, she became angry. "What's that you say?" she shrieked, and swung at the smith with the ladle.

"Hang on, if you want to come along!" said Taper-Tom; so she stuck fast, she too; and for all she scolded, and for all she tugged and tore, and as wild as she was, she had to hobble along. But, when they came outside the front window, the princess stood and waited for them, and when she saw that they had the cook along, with both ladle and pot, she burst out laughing, and laughed so hard that the king had to hold her up. So Taper-Tom got the princess and half the kingdom, and they held a wedding so grand that it was the talk of the whole land.

THE CHARCOAL BURNER

There was once a charcoal burner who had a son, and the son was a charcoal burner, too. When the father had died, the son took a wife, but he wouldn't do any work; poor he was at looking after the kiln, too, and at last nobody wanted to hire him to burn charcoal any more. But one day he did manage to burn a kiln full, and went to town with some loads of charcoal to sell. When he had sold them, he rambled along the main street and had a look around. On his way home he joined company with neighbors and parish folk, and reveled and drank and chattered about all the things he had seen in town. The funniest thing he had seen, he said, was that there were so many parsons there, and everybody greeted them and tipped their hats at them. "I wish I were a parson, too, for then people might tip their hats at me. Now they mostly act as though they didn't see me," he said.

Drawings by Erik Werenskiold

"Well, you're *black* enough if nothing else to be a parson," said the neighbors to the charcoal burner. "But as long as we're on our way anyhow, we can go to the auction of the late parson's things and get ourselves a drop of something, and at the same time you can buy the cassock and ruff," they said. Well, that's what they did, and when he got home he hadn't a shilling left.

"I hope you have both food and money with you," said the wife.

"Yes, now there'll be food, mother," said the charcoal burner, "for I've become a parson!" he said. "Here you see both the cassock and the ruff."

"That I'm likely to believe! Strong ale makes for brave words!" said the old woman. "It makes no difference to you which end is up," she said.

"Never blame nor praise the kiln before the coals have cooled," said the charcoal burner.

Then came a day when so many clergymen, in cassocks and ruff collars, passed the charcoal burner's place on the way to the king's manor that they could tell something was to happen there. Well, the charcoal burner wanted to go along too, and dressed himself in his clerical garments. The old woman thought it would be just as well if he stayed at home, for if he were to hold a horse for a fine gentleman, he'd just drink up the tip he got for it.

"Everybody talks about the drink, but nobody about the thirst, mother," he said, and strode to the king's manor.

There all the strangers were invited in, and the charcoal burner went in too. Now the king told them that he had lost the costliest of all his rings, and he was quite certain it had been stolen. So he had summoned all the learned clergymen in the land on the chance that they could tell him who the thief was. And he promised that he would reward the one who could: if it were someone studying to become a parson, he would get a parsonage; if he were already a parson, he should be made a dean; if he were a dean, he would be made a bishop; and if he were a bishop, he would be next in rank to the king himself. Then the king went from one to the other and questioned them all, and when he came to the charcoal burner he said, "Who are you?"

"I am the wise parson and the true prophet," answered the charcoal burner.

"Then you can surely tell me who has stolen my ring," said the king.

"Well, it's not good sense to think that what is hidden in darkness should now be visible in daylight," said the charcoal burner. "But it's not every year that the salmon spawns in the top of a spruce tree. Now I've been studying for seven years for me and mine, but I have no parish of my own yet. So if I am to bring the thief to light, I must have a lot of time and plenty of paper, for I have to write and reckon through many a land."

Well, he was promised plenty of time and all the paper he wanted if only he could produce the thief. He was given a room to himself in the king's manor, and it didn't take long before everybody realized that he must know more than the Lord's Prayer, for he used up so much paper that it lay in great heaps and piles. But there wasn't one of them who could understand a word of what he had written, because it looked like nothing but scrawls and pothooks. Time

26

went on, and still he could say nothing about the thief. At last the king grew tired of it, and told him that if he could not find the thief in three days, he would lose his life.

"The one who is to rule must not be too hasty. One shouldn't rake out the coal before the kiln is cold," said the charcoal burner. But the king was firm, and the charcoal burner realized that his life was not worth much after that.

Now, three of the king's servants had been appointed to wait on the charcoal burner, one each day. And it was these three who had banded together to steal the king's

They went in and fell on their knees before the charcoal burner, and begged him, for heaven's sake, not to tell the king.

ring. When one of the servants came in and cleared off the table after supper, the charcoal burner sighed deeply and looked at him. "That was the first," he said, meaning that it was the first of the three days he had left of his life.

"This parson knows about more than just eating," said the servant when he had his comrades by themselves, and then he told them he had said "That was the first." The second, who was to wait on the parson the next day, was told to listen carefully to what he said, and sure enough, when he had cleared the table and was going out after supper, the charcoal burner stared hard at him, sighed deeply, and said, "That was the second." The third one was told to pay very close attention to the way the charcoal burner behaved on the third day, and it was no better; for when the servant took hold of the doorknob, and was about to leave with cups and plates, the charcoal burner folded his hands and said, "*That was the third!*" And then he sighed as though his heart would break.

When the servant got outside, he was so frightened he could hardly breathe, and he told the others that it was quite clear that the parson knew. So they went in and fell on their knees before the charcoal burner, and begged him, for heaven's sake, not to tell the king. They would each gladly give him a hundred *dalers*, if he would save them from certain death. He promised sure and certain that he would not tell on them if they would give him the money and the ring, and a big lump of porridge as well. Then the parson rolled the ring well inside the lump of porridge, and told one of them to give it to the biggest hog in the king's barn, and watch that the hog didn't drop it.

The next morning the king came. He was in a difficult mood, and wanted to know at once who the thief was.

"Well, now that I have reckoned and written through many a land," said the charcoal burner, "I know it's not a human being who has stolen your ring."

"Nonsense! Who *has* stolen it, then?" asked the king.

"Oh, it's the big hog in your barn," said the charcoal burner. Well, they butchered the hog, and sure enough, in its belly they found the ring.

Then the charcoal burner was made a parson, and the king was so pleased that he gave him a horse and a manor, and a hundred *dalers* besides. The charcoal burner wasted no time moving in, and on the first Sunday after he had been made a parson, he was to go to church and read his letter of appointment. But before he left home he had to have lunch, so he put the letter beside him on a piece of bread. But then he dipped the letter in the broth, mistaking it for the slice of bread, and when he found it tough to chew on, he threw it to the dog, who gobbled it up in no time.

Now he didn't know what he was going to do, but to church he had to go, for the parishoners were waiting. And when he got there, he went straight up into the pulpit. There he started puffing himself up so that everyone thought he was indeed a fine parson. But after a while, he didn't seem so fine any more.

"My listeners, the words you should have heard today have gone to the dogs. But come back another Sunday, my dear parishoners, and you shall hear something different. And with this, my sermon for today is ended."

The congregation thought this was a very strange parson, for such a sermon they had never heard before; but then they thought he might improve, and if he didn't, there would always be a way to have things changed.

On the next Sunday there was another service, and the church was so full of people who wanted to listen to the new parson that there was hardly room for them all inside. Well, when he came, he went straight up into the pulpit where he stood for a while without saying a word. Then he banged on the pulpit and shouted, "Listen, you old Buck-Berit, why do you sit so far back in the church?"

"I have such trashy shoes, father," she said.

"Oh, you could take an old sow hide and make yourself a pair of shoes so you could sit just as far up in the church as the other respectable women. Furthermore, all of you should bear in mind what road you are following, for I

28

see, when I come to church, that some come from the north and some from the south, and it's the same when you leave the church again. But you must stop, and then the question is: what will become of you? Who knows what will become of any one of us? — And now I have to announce that a black mare has got away from our former parson's wife. She has a fetlock and a hanging mane, and more like that, which I shan't mention in this place. — And then I have a hole in the pocket of my old breeches; that I know, but not you; but if anyone has a patch which could fit the hole, neither you nor I know it."

Some of the parishoners were pretty well pleased with the sermon. They could not but think that he would be a good parson in time, they said. But most of them felt it was much too bad, and when the time came for the dean's visit, they complained about the parson and said that no one had ever heard such sermons before, and one of them recalled the last one, and repeated it to the dean.

That was a very good sermon, said the dean, for it was only to be assumed that the parson had spoken in parables about seeking divine light and fleeing darkness and its evils, and about those who went on the broad and the narrow paths. The reference to the old parson's black mare was an excellent parable about what would happen to us all at the end; and as to the hole in his pocket, that was to express his need, and the patch was to signify offerings and charity which he expected from the congregation, explained the dean.

"Well, that much we understood, too, that it was the parson's moneybag," they thought. At last the dean said he thought the congregation had got such a fine and intelligent man for a parson, that they ought not complain about him. And in the end they didn't get another. But, as they thought things were growing worse and not better, they complained to the bishop.

Well, he came at last, and he was to conduct the service. But the day before, the charcoal burner had gone to the church when no one knew about it, and sawed loose the pulpit so that it only just didn't collapse when one climbed carefully into it. When the congregation had taken their seats, and it was time for the charcoal burner to preach for the bishop, he tiptoed into the pulpit, and started preaching in his usual manner. But when he had been preaching for a little while, he became more and more excited, threw up his arms and shouted, "If there is anyone here who has a bad conscience for something evil he has done, he had better leave this church, for on this day will occur a mighty fall, unequalled by anything that has happened since the creation of this world." With that he struck the pulpit a thunderous blow, and pulpit and parson and all fell down with a terrible crash, and the whole congregation ran out of the church as though the Day of Judgement had come.

But now the bishop told the congregation that he was surprised that they could complain of a parson who was so gifted, and had such wisdom that he could predict things to come. He thought the parson ought at least to be a dean, he said; and it wasn't long, either, before he was. So there was no way out, they were saddled with him.

Now, the king and the queen had no children, but when the king learned that perhaps one was on the way, he was anxious to know whether the child would be an heir to land and kingdom, or merely a princess. So all the learned men in the kingdom were summoned to the palace to see if they could tell what the child was to be. But as none of them could answer that question, both the king and the bishop remembered the charcoal burner, and it wasn't long before they got him to the manor, where they tried to get him to give an opinion. But no, he couldn't help them, either, he said, for it is not for anyone to guess what no one could know.

"That's all very well," said the king. "I don't care whether you *know* it or not, but you are supposed to be the wise parson and true prophet who can predict things to come, and if you won't tell us, you shall loose both cassock and collar," said the king. "I shall put you to a test first," he said, and then he took the largest silver beaker he owned, and went down to the shore. "If you can tell me what is in this beaker," said the king, "you can also tell me about the child." And he held the lid on the beaker.

The charcoal burner wrung his hands and carried on badly. "Oh, you most miserable, creeping crab on this earth, what have you now for all your toiling and moiling?" he said.

"Well, see if you didn't know it!" said the king, for he had a big crab in the beaker. So the charcoal burner had to go into the front room to the queen. He took a chair and sat down in the middle of the floor, and the queen walked back and forth in front of the room.

"One should never build a stall for an unborn calf, nor argue about the name before the child is born," said the charcoal burner. "But never have I seen anything like this before," he said. "When the queen walks towards me it looks as if it will be a prince, and when she walks away from me, it looks as if it were a princess."

In due time the queen gave birth to twins, so the charcoal burner had hit the nail on the head this time, too. And because he could tell what no one else knew, he was given money by the wagon-load, and then he became the highest person next to the king.

Trip, trap, trill, he got more than his fill.

THE THREE PRINCESSES
IN THE MOUNTAIN-IN-THE-BLUE

There were once a king and a queen who had no children, and they took it so to heart that they hardly ever had a happy moment.

One day the king was standing on the porch of his house, looking out over his broad acres and everything he owned. There was plenty, and well it looked, too; but he did not feel that he could enjoy it, as long as he did not know what would become of it all after his death. As he stood there pondering, up came a poor old woman who went around begging for a pittance in God's name. She greeted him and curtsied, and asked what ailed the king since he looked so unhappy.

"Nothing you can do anything about, my good woman!" said the king. "There's no use telling you."

Drawings by Erik Werenskiold

"There just might be," said the beggar woman. "A mere trifle is often enough when luck is on your side. The king is thinking that he has no heir to his land and kingdom, but he need not grieve over that," she said. She told him his queen would have three daughters, but he must take good care never to let them out into the open before they were fifteen years old, or else a snowflurry would come and take them.

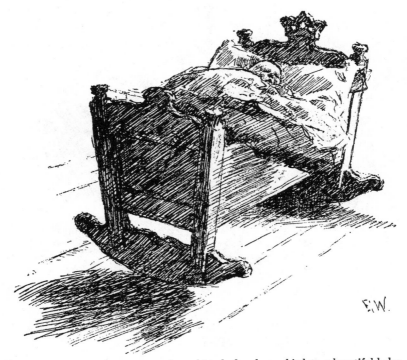

When her time came, the queen was brought to bed and gave birth to a beautiful baby girl.

When her time came, the queen was brought to bed and gave birth to a beautiful baby girl. The following year she had a second daughter, and the third year one more. The king and the queen were happy beyond words, but for all his joy, the king remembered to place a guard at the hall door so that the princesses would not be able to go outside.

As the princesses grew, they became both pretty and graceful, and they were happy in every way, except for the fact that they were never allowed to go outside and play like other children. But for all they begged and pleaded with their parents, and for all they pestered the guard, they were told they must not go out before all three of them were fifteen years old.

One day, not long before the youngest princess reached her fifteenth birthday, the king and the queen were out driving in the fine weather, and the princesses were standing at the window gazing out. The sun was shining, and everything was so green and pretty that they felt they *had* to go out — come what might! So they begged and pestered the guard, and pleaded with him to let them go out into the garden. He could see for himself how warm and sunny it was — winter weather could never come on such a day.

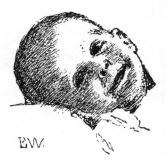

No, that didn't seem very likely to the guard, either; and if they really insisted on going outside, they might as well, he said. But only for a tiny, little while; and he would go with them himself, and keep an eye on them.

When they came into the garden, they ran hither and thither, and picked armfuls of flowers and greenery — they had never set eyes on anything so lovely. At last they couldn't pick any more, but just as they were to go inside again, they caught sight of a big rose at the other end of the garden. It was far, far lovelier than any of the other flowers they had found, so they simply had to have it. But at the very moment they leaned over to pick the rose, a big snowflurry came, and they were gone.

There was great sorrow throughout the land, and the king had it proclaimed in all the churches that the one who could rescue the princesses should get half the kingdom, and his golden crown, and whichever of them he wanted for a wife. There were plenty who wanted to win half a kingdom and a princess into the bargain, you may be sure, and high-born and lowborn set out and searched in every corner of the land. But there was not one who could find the king's daughters, or even so much as a trace of them.

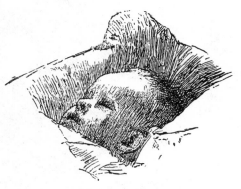

Now, when all the high and mighty in the land had searched in vain, there were a captain and a lieutenant who wanted to try their luck. Well, the king furnished them with both silver and gold, and wished them God-speed into the bargain.

Then there was a soldier who lived with his mother in a little cottage just beyond the king's manor. He dreamed one night that he, too, was setting out to look for the princesses. In the morning he remembered what he had dreamed, and told his mother about it.

33

So they begged and pestered the guard.

"It may just be some witchcraft that has come your way," said the old woman. "You must dream the same dream three nights in a row, or else it doesn't count."

But the two following nights the same thing happened as on the first: both times he had the same dream again, and he felt he had to go out.

So he washed himself and put on his uniform, and went up to the kitchen of the king's manor. It was the day after the captain and the lieutenant had set out.

"You go home again," said the king. "The princesses are too far above you," he said. "And besides, I've given out so much travel money that there's no more left today. You'd better come back another day."

"If I'm going, I'll go today," said the soldier. "I need no travel money. I

A little cottage just beyond the king's manor.

don't want anything more than a dram in my flask and food in my knapsack," he said. But he must have plenty in his knapsack, as much beef and pork as he could carry.

Well, he would get that as long as there was nothing else he wanted.

So he set off on the way, and he hadn't gone many miles before he caught up with the captain and the lieutenant.

"Where are you off to?" asked the captain when he saw the uniform.

"I'm going out to try and find the king's daughters," replied the soldier.

"So are we," said the captain, "and as long as you're on the same errand, you may as well come with us. After all, if we don't find them, then *you* certainly won't find them either, my boy!" he said.

After they had been walking together for a while, the soldier turned off the highway along a footpath leading into the forest.

"Hey! Where are you going?" said the captain. "It's best to stick to the highway!" he said.

"So it would seem," said the soldier. "But this is the way I'm going."

He kept to the path, he did, and when the others saw that, they turned off the highway and came after him. The path took them away through the woods, over great moors and up narrow, out-of-the-way valleys. At last they saw daylight, and when they were out of the forest, they came to a long, long footbridge which they had to cross, and on that bridge stood a bear on guard. It reared up on its hind legs and came towards them as though it wanted to eat them.

35

In the evening they came to a large and splendid manor.

"What'll we do now?" said the captain.

"They say the bear is supposed to be wild about beef," said the soldier, and threw it a haunch.

In this way they managed to get past. But at the other end of the bridge stood a lion, and it roared and rushed at them with gaping jaws as though it were going to devour them.

"Now we'd better turn our noses homeward! We'll never get past here alive," said the captain.

"Oh, he can't be so dangerous either," said the soldier. "I've heard the lion is supposed to be crazy about pork, and in the knapsack I've got half a pig," he said. So he threw a ham to the lion, and it started gnawing and eating, and so they got past that place too.

In the evening they came to a large and splendid manor. Each room was finer than the next, and wherever they looked, it sparkled and shone. But that was not going to fill anyone's belly, I can tell you. The captain and the lieutenant went about jingling their money, and would gladly have bought themselves something to eat. But not a soul did they see, nor a crumb of food did they find. So the soldier offered them beef and pork from his knapsack, and they soon pocketed their pride and fell to with a will. They helped themselves to what he had, as though they had never tasted food before.

*   *   *

The next day the captain said they would have to go hunting and get themselves something to live on. Close to the manor was a dense forest, full of rabbits and wild fowl. The lieutenant was to stay at home and mind the house, and cook the rest of the provisions. In the meantime, the two others killed so much game that it was all they could do to carry it home. But when they came to the gate, the lieutenant was so feeble that he could hardly open it for them.

"What's happened to you?" asked the captain.

Well, he told them that as soon as they had gone, there came a tiny little fellow, with a long, long beard, walking on crutches, and begging so piteously

36

for a penny. But no sooner had he got it than it fell on the floor, and for all he scrambled after it, he just couldn't get hold of it, so stiff and crooked was he.

"I felt sorry for the old creature," said the lieutenant, "so I bent down to pick up the penny. But all of a sudden he was neither stiff nor feeble any longer. He started using his crutches on me until I could hardly stir a limb."

"You ought to be ashamed of yourself, you one of the king's men, letting an old cripple give you a thrashing — and talking about it into the bargain!" said the captain. "Pooh! Tomorrow I'll stay at home. Then it'll be another story!"

Next day the lieutenant and the soldier went hunting, and the captain stayed at home to cook the food and mind the house. But if he fared no worse, he certainly fared no better. As the day wore on, the old fellow turned up and begged for a penny. He dropped it as soon as he got it; and it was nowhere to be found. So he asked the captain to help him find it, and *he* had no better sense than to stoop down and look for it. But hardly had he bent down before the old fellow started whacking him with the crutches. And every time the captain tried to get up and hit back, he received such a blow that stars danced before his eyes. When the others came home in the evening, he was still lying in the same spot with a vacant look on his face.

On the third day the soldier was to stay at home while the two others went hunting. The captain told him to take good care, "for the old fellow will certainly beat you to death, my boy!" he said.

"Oh, I'm too fond of life to let an old cripple deprive me of it," thought the soldier.

They were no sooner out of the gate than the old fellow was there begging for a penny again.

"Money I've never had," said the soldier, "but food you shall have as soon as it's ready," he said. "But if we're going to get a fire going, you must chop some wood."

"I can't," said the fellow.

"If you can't then you can certainly learn," said the soldier. "That's soon done. Just come along down to the woodshed."

There he dragged out a huge log, cut a crack in it, and drove in a wedge so that it became a long, deep split.

"Now you must lie down and sight carefully along the crack. Then you'll soon learn how to chop wood," said the soldier. "In the meantime, I'll start chopping."

Well, the old fellow was fool enough to do as he was told: he lay down and sighted along the log. When the soldier saw that his beard was well down in the crack, he knocked out the wedge and started soundly thrashing the fellow with the axe handle. Then he swung the axe over his head and swore he would split his skull if he didn't tell him that very instant where the king's daughters were.

"Spare my life! Spare my life! I'll tell you!" shouted the fellow. "East of the manor there's a big mound," he said. "On top of the mound you're to dig

But if he fared no worse, he certainly fared no better.

loose a square piece of turf. Then you'll see a huge slab of rock, and under it is a deep hole. You must lower yourself down the hole. Then you'll come to another world, and there you'll find the princesses with the Mountain Trolls. But it's deep, and it's dark down there, and you must pass through both water and fire."

When the soldier had found out what he wanted to know, he released the old fellow from the log, and *he* wasn't slow in bidding farewell.

When the captain and the lieutenant came home, they were amazed to find the soldier alive. Well, he told them how he had fared from first to last, and where the king's daughters were, and how they were to find them. They were as happy as though they had already found them, and when they had had some food, they took a basket and all the rope and cord they could find, and went to the mound — all three of them. There they first cut loose the turf, just as the fellow had said. Underneath they found a great big stone slab, and it was all they could do to roll it aside. Then they tried to find out how deep the hole was. They tied the pieces of rope together, first two lengths and then three, but they found no more bottom the last time than the first. At last they had to tie together all the pieces they had, both thick and thin; then they felt it reach all the way to the bottom.

The captain wanted to be the first to descend, you may be sure. "But when I tug on the rope, you must be quick and haul me up again," he said.

The hole was both dark and dismal, but he thought he had better go through with it, as long as it got no worse. But all at once cold water started spouting about his ears; at that he was frightened to death and started tugging on the rope.

Then the lieutenant wanted to try, but he didn't fare much better. When he was well past the flood of water, he caught sight of flames blazing away below him, and he was so frightened that he, too, had to turn around and return to the top of the shaft.

Then the soldier climbed into the basket. He kept going through both fire and water, all the way to the bottom. Down there it was so pitch black that he could not see his hand in front of his nose. Nor did he dare let go the basket either, but went round in a circle groping and fumbling about.

Then he caught sight of a tiny glimmer of light a long, long way off, just like the dawn. He walked toward it, and when he had gone part of the way it started growing brighter about him, and it wasn't long before he saw a golden sun rise in the heavens, and the daylight was as bright and clear as in the real world. First he came to a great herd of cattle, with cows so fat and sleek that they glistened. And when he had passed them, he came to a large and splendid castle.

There he walked through many rooms before he met anyone. At last he heard the whirring of a spinning wheel, and when he went in, there sat the king's eldest daughter spinning copper yarn; and the room and everything in it were of burnished copper.

"My! Have Christian folk come here?" exclaimed the princess. "Lord have mercy upon you! What do you want here?"

"I want to rescue you from the mountain," replied the soldier.

"My good fellow, begone! If the Troll comes home, he'll put an end to you right away. He has three heads!" she said.

"I don't care if he has four!" said the soldier. "Now that I've come, I'm going to stay!"

"Well, since you're so stubborn, I suppose I'd better see if I can help you," said the king's daughter. Then she told him to crawl behind the big brewing vat which stood out in the hall. In the meantime, she would make the Troll welcome, and stroke his heads until he fell asleep. "Then, when I go out and call in the hens, you must come in as quickly as you can," she said. "Now go out and try to swing the sword that's lying on the table."

But the sword was too heavy; he couldn't so much as budge it. So he had to take a strength-giving draught from the drinking-horn that was hanging behind the hall door. Then he could just raise the sword from the table. He took another swig, and now he could lift it; so he took a really big one, and was able to swing the sword as easily as could be.

All at once the Troll came rushing in with a noise that shook the castle.

"Fie! Fie! I smell the blood and bones of a Christian in my house!" he said.

39

"Yes, a raven flew past just now," said the king's daughter, "and it had a man's bone in its beak, which it dropped down the chimney. I threw it out, right away, and swept up after it, too, but I suppose it still smells."

"I can smell it, all right!" said the Troll.

"But come now, I'm going to stroke your heads," said the princess. "Then it'll be better when you wake up."

The Troll agreed right away, and it wasn't long before he was so sound asleep that he snored. When she saw that he had fallen asleep, she propped up his heads with chairs and quilts, and started calling the hens. Then the soldier tip-toed in with the sword, and cut off all three of the Troll's heads with a single blow.

The princess was as merry as a fiddle, and went along with him to her sisters so that he could rescue them from the mountain too. First they crossed a court-yard, and then passed through many great halls until they came to a huge door.

"This is where you must go in," said the princess. "Here it is."

When he opened the door, he saw a great hall, and everything inside was of the finest silver. There sat the middle sister spinning on a silver spinning wheel.

"Oh, save you!" she said. "What do you want here?"

"To rescue you from the Troll," said the soldier.

"My good fellow, begone!" said the princess. "If he finds you here, he'll take your life on the spot!"

"That's too bad — but suppose I take *his* first!" said the soldier.

"Well, if you really *want* to," she said, "then you must crawl behind the big vat out in the hall. But you must hurry and come as soon as you hear me calling the hens."

But first he had to see if he were strong enough to swing the Troll-sword which lay on the table. It was much bigger and heavier than the first one, and it was all he could do to budge it. So he took three swigs from the horn, and then he was able to lift it. And when he had taken three more, he could brandish it as though it were a pancake turner.

After a short while there was a terrible rumbling and crashing, and immediately after, in came a Troll with six heads!

"Fie! Fie!" he said, as soon as he had put his noses inside the door. "I smell the blood and bones of a Christian in my house!"

"Yes, just fancy, a little while ago a raven came flying past with a thigh-bone, and dropped it down the chimney!" said the king's daughter. "I threw it out, and the raven dropped it down the chimney again. At last I got rid of it. and hurried to smoke the smell out, but it still seems to be lingering," she said.

"I can smell it, all right!" said the Troll.

But he was tired, so he laid his heads in the princess's lap, and she stroked them until all the heads were snoring. Then she called in the hens, and the soldier came and chopped off all six heads as though they were growing on cabbage stalks.

She was no less happy than her sister, as you can imagine; but in the midst of their dancing and singing they remembered their youngest sister, and so they led the soldier across one more large courtyard, and through a great many rooms, until he came to the third princess in the golden hall.

She was sitting, spinning golden yarn on a golden spinning wheel, and from floor to ceiling the room glittered so that it hurt to look at it.

"Preserve and help both you and me!" said the princess who was sitting there. "Go! Go! Or else he'll kill us both!"

"Just as well two as one," said the soldier.

The princess wept and pleaded, but it was not the slightest use. He had made up his mind to stay, and that was that! As there was no other way out, she told him to try the Troll-sword out on the table in the hall. But he could only just budge it — it was even bigger and heavier than the other two. So he had to take down the drinking-horn from the wall, and take three swigs from it. But even then he could only just lift the sword. When he had taken three more strength-giving swigs, he swung it as easily as a feather. Then she made the same plan with the soldier as her two sisters had made: when the Troll had fallen fast asleep, she would call in the hens, and then he must come quickly and do away with him.

All at once there was a booming and a shaking as though the walls and ceiling were about to fall down.

"Fie! Fie! I smell the blood and bones of a Christian in my house!" said the Troll, sniffing the air with all his nine noses.

"Yes, would you believe it! Just now a raven flew past and dropped a man's bone down the chimney. I threw it out, and the raven threw it in, and back and forth it went," said the princess. But in the end she had buried it, she said, and had aired the room thoroughly, but a little of the odor still lingered.

"I can smell it, all right," said the Troll.

"Come here and lay your heads in my lap," said the princess. "Then it'll probably be better after you've had a nap."

He did just as she said, and when he was snoring like a beast, she propped up the heads with benches and quilts so that she could get away, and started calling the hens. Then the soldier tiptoed in in his stockinged feet, and struck out at the Troll so that eight heads flew off at the same time — the sword was too short and didn't reach any farther.

The ninth head woke up and started roaring, "Fie! Fie! I smell a Christian here!"

"Yes, and here *is* the Christian!" replied the soldier, and before the Troll could get up and grab hold of him, the soldier gave one more blow so that the last head rolled off.

You may be sure the princesses were glad now that they didn't have to sit and scratch the Trolls' heads any longer; there was no end to the kindnesses they wanted to do for the man who had freed them, and the youngest princess wrenched off her golden ring and knotted it into his hair. Then they

41

gathered up as much gold and silver as they thought they could carry, and started for home.

As soon as they tugged on the rope, the captain and the lieutenant hauled up the princesses one after the other. But when they were safely up, the soldier realized that he had been foolish not to seat himself in the basket and go up ahead of the princesses, for he didn't trust his comrades at all. Now he decided to try them, so he put a huge lump of gold in the basket and jumped to one side. When it was a good halfway up, they cut the rope so that the basket crashed down on to the rock and the pieces flew about his ears.

"Now we're rid of him!" they said. Then they threatened to kill the princesses if they didn't say that *they* were the ones that had rescued them from the Trolls. The princesses didn't like it one bit, especially the youngest one; but life is precious, so the captain and the lieutenant had it their own way.

Now when the captain and the lieutenant came home with the princesses, there was indeed great rejoicing at the king's manor. The king was so happy that he didn't know which foot to stand on. He took his best bottle of wine out of the cupboard and poured out a cup of welcome for the two of them; and if they hadn't been made much of before, they were now, I can tell you. And they strutted back and forth, and preened themselves like gentlemen the whole day, now that they were getting the king himself for a father-in-law; for it was clear that each would wed a princess — whichever one he wanted — and that they would divide half the kingdom between them. They both wanted the youngest, but for all they begged and threatened, they got nowhere. She wouldn't have them in any shape or form. So they talked to the king about setting twelve men to guard her; she had been so gloomy ever since she had been in the mountain, they said, and they were afraid she might do herself some harm.

This the king agreed to do; and he told the guard to take good care of her, and to follow her wherever she went day and night.

And now a feast was to be prepared for the two eldest princesses, with much brewing and baking. This was to be a wedding the like of which had never before been seen nor heard of; and they brewed, and they baked, and they butchered as though it would never come to an end.

In the meantime, the soldier wandered aimlessly back and forth in the other world. He was sad to think that he would never again see a human face nor the light of day; but he had to keep himself busy with something, he thought, and so he went from room to room, one day and two days and many more. He rummaged in all the cupboards and drawers, and poked about in the shelves, and looked at all the fine things that were there. After a while he came to a drawer in a table; he pulled it out, and inside lay a golden key. So he tried the key in all the locks there were, but not one did it fit until he came to a little wall cupboard over the bed, and in that he found a rusty old whistle.

"It might be worth trying to see if there's any sound in it," he thought, and put it to his mouth. Before he knew what was happening, there was a whirring

42

and a rushing on all sides, and, all of a sudden, down swooped a flock of birds so large that the ground was black.

"What does our master wish today?" they asked.

Well, if *he* were their master, said the soldier, then he'd certainly like to know if they could tell him how to get back to the earth.

No, there was not one who could, "— but our mother hasn't come yet," they said. "If she can't help you, then there's no way!"

So he blew the whistle once more, and after a little while he heard something beating its wings a long way off. At the same time a wind started blowing so hard that he was thrown from one wall of the courtyard to another like a wisp of hay, and if he hadn't grabbed hold of the rail fence he would almost certainly have blown away at once. Thereupon an eagle glided down in front of him, so big that it was beyond words to describe.

"You come hard, you do!" said the soldier.

"I come the way you blow!" said the eagle.

Then he asked if she knew of a way for him to escape out of the world they were in now.

"Nestlings can't get away from here," said the eagle, "but if you'll slaughter twelve oxen for me, so that I can eat my fill, I'll try to help you, I will! Have you a knife?"

"No, but I have a sword," said the soldier.

When the eagle had finished off the twelve oxen, she bade him slaughter one more and take it along as provisions for the journey. "Every time I open my beak, you must be quick and throw a piece in," she said, "or else I won't be able to carry you aloft."

Well, he did as she asked, and hung two big sacks of meat around her neck; and he snuggled down among her feathers. Then the eagle flapped her wings, and with that they were off like a wind so that the air whistled past. The soldier had all he could do to hold on tight, and it was only by the skin of his teeth that he managed to fling the pieces of meat into the eagle's beak each time she opened it. At last daylight began to glimmer above them; but now the eagle was losing speed and began fluttering her wings. The soldier was ready, and grabbed the last haunch and threw it to her. Then she got back her strength and flew on. And after she had sat and rested for a while in the top of a big fir tree, she set off with him again so fast that they flashed past land and sea, wherever they went. Close by the king's manor he climbed down, and the eagle flew home again; but first she said that if there was anything he wanted, he had only to blow the whistle and she would come at once.

In the meantime, everything was in readiness at the king's manor, and the day was approaching when the captain and the lieutenant were to wed the two eldest princesses. But *they* were not much happier than the youngest sister. Never a day went by that they didn't grieve and cry, and the closer they came to the wedding day, the sadder they grew. At last the king asked what was wrong with them. He thought it more than strange that they were not happy and gay now that they were free and saved, and were to be married as well. They had to say something, so the eldest princess said they would never be happy again if they couldn't get a board-game like the one they had played with in the Mountain-in-the-Blue.

The king thought he could certainly get one for them, so he sent word to all the best and most skilled goldsmiths in the land to make a board-game of gold for the princesses. But, for all they tried, there was not one who was able to make such a game.

At last all the goldsmiths in the land had been asked save one, and he was a feeble old man who hadn't turned out a proper piece of work for many a year, but only tinkered with a little silver work — just enough to keep himself alive. So the soldier went and apprenticed himself to him, and the old man was so happy to get an apprentice — he hadn't had one for a year and a day — that he dug out a flask from his cupboard and sat down to drink with the soldier. It wasn't long before the spirits had gone to his head, and when the soldier saw that, he persuaded the smith to go to the king and tell him that he could make the game for the princesses. The old man agreed to this on the spot, for he had made things just as fine and fancy in his day, he had!

When the king heard there was someone outside who could make a copy of the board-game, he wasn't slow in coming out.

"Is it true, what they say, that you can make a game like the one my daughters want?" he asked.

Yes, that was quite true, replied the smith, and he stuck to his story.

"That's good," said the king. "Here is some gold for you to make it from. But if you fail, you shall lose your life, seeing that you have come forward of your own accord!" And the old man was given three days to make the game in.

Next morning, when the goldsmith had slept off his befuddlement, he wasn't anywhere near so proud. He cried and carried on, and swore at his apprentice who had caused him to get himself into mischief while he was tipsy. Now the only way out would be for him to do away with himself right away, for there was no point in pleading for his life. If the most skillful goldsmiths couldn't make such a game, it wasn't likely that *he* could manage it.

"Don't worry about that, just hand over the gold," said the soldier. "I'll get the game all right. But I want a room to myself to work in," he said.

This he got, and the old man's thanks into the bargain.

But time dragged on and on, and he did nothing, and the goldsmith went about moaning because he would never get on with his task.

"Never bother yourself about *that*," said the soldier. "It's a long time to the hour. If you're not satisfied with what I've promised, you can make the game yourself!"

It was the same tale that day and the next; and when the smith heard neither hammer nor file from his room all the last day either, he gave up all hope; for now there was no longer any chance of saving his life, he thought.

But as night drew on, the soldier opened his window and blew his whistle.

Yes, that was quite true, replied the smith, and he stuck to his story.

"Out in the barn I've got a couple of ox carcasses for you," said the soldier.

In a trice the eagle appeared, and asked what he wanted.

"The golden board-game which the princesses used in the Mountain-in-the-Blue," said the soldier. "But no doubt you want something to eat first? Out in the barn I've got a couple of ox carcasses for you. You can have them," he said.

When the eagle had eaten them, she didn't lose much time, and long before the sun rose she was back with the game. Then the soldier put it under his bed, and lay down to sleep.

At the crack of dawn next morning the goldsmith came and pounded on his door.

"You've been doing quite a bit of running," said the soldier. "All day you've rushed around as if you were completely mad. If I'm not going to be allowed to have a night's rest, you'll have to get another apprentice!"

But this time neither pleading nor praying was any use; the goldsmith insisted on being admitted, and at last he pushed up the latch.

And you can imagine that there was an end to his whining!

But even more delighted than the goldsmith were the princesses, when he came up to the king's manor with the game; and most delighted of them all was the youngest princess.

"Have you made that game yourself?" she asked.

"No, to tell the truth I haven't," he said. "It's an apprentice I have."

"I would like to see that apprentice," said the princess.

46

"Good day, how nice to see you again!" said the youngest princess.

All three of them wanted to meet him, and, if he valued his life, he had better come.

The soldier feared neither lords nor ladies, and if it gave them any pleasure to look at his rags, they might as well have their wish gratified.

The king's youngest daughter knew him again right away; she pushed aside the guard, ran over and offered him her hand, and said, "Good day, how nice to see you again." Then she said to the king, "Here's the man who rescued us from the Trolls in the mountain! He's the one I want to marry!" And she swept off his cap and showed them the ring she had fastened in his hair.

Well, then the full story of the way the captain and the lieutenant had carried on came to light. They had to pay for it with their lives, and that was the end of them.

But the soldier got the golden crown, and half the kingdom, and wed the king's youngest daughter. And at the wedding they drank and reveled both long and merrily, for all who were there could revel — even if they couldn't all rescue the king's daughters.

And if they haven't drunk their fill, they must be sitting and drinking and reveling still!

THE GOLDEN BIRD

There was once a king who had a garden. In that garden stood an apple tree, and on that tree there grew, each year, a golden apple. But when the time came to pick it, it was gone; nobody knew who had taken it nor what had become of it, but gone it was.

This king had three sons. So one day he told them that the one who could recover the apple or catch the thief should inherit the kingdom after him, no matter whether he was the eldest, the youngest or the middle one.

The eldest brother set out first, and sat down under the tree to wait for the thief. As night was drawing near, a golden bird came flying, and it shone from afar. But, when the king's son saw the bird and the light, he became so frightened that he dared not stay but ran home as fast as his legs would carry him.

In the morning the apple had disappeared. But now the king's son had regained his courage, and so he started fitting himself out, for he wanted to go away to look for the golden bird. The king equipped him well and spared neither clothes nor money.

Drawings by Th. Kittelsen

When the king's son had travelled a while he became hungry, and, taking up his knapsack, he sat down by the roadside and started to eat. Just then a fox came out from a grove of fir trees and sat down and looked at him.

"Pray give me a little food," said the fox.

"I'll give you some burnt horn!" said the king's son. "I need all the food for myself, as nobody knows how far or how long I shall have to travel."

"Well, that was that!" said the fox, and then he went back to the woods again.

When the prince had eaten and rested, he continued on his way. After a while he came to a big city, and in that city was an inn where there was always great merriment and never sorrow. This must be a fine place to stay, thought the prince to himself, so he remained there. And there was so much dancing and drinking, and pleasure and fun, that he forgot all about the golden bird, and the apple, and his father and the journey, and the whole kingdom. Gone he was and gone he stayed.

The next year the middle son was to try to catch the apple thief in the garden. Well, he sat under the tree too, when the apple was almost ripe. And all at once the golden bird came one night, shining like a sun, but the boy became so frightened that he took to his heels and ran home as fast as he could.

The following morning the apple was gone; but by now the king's son had regained his courage, and wanted to set out to see if he could find the bird. So he started fitting himself out, and the king equipped him well, and spared neither clothes nor money.

But the same thing happened to him as to his elder brother: when he had travelled a while he became hungry, and, taking up his knapsack, he sat down to have lunch by the side of the road. Then a fox came out from a grove of fir trees and sat down to watch.

"Pray give me a little food!" said the fox.

"I'll give you burnt horn, I will!" said the king's son. "Nobody knows how far or how long I shall have to travel, so I need all the food for myself."

"Well, that was that!" said the fox, and then he went back to the woods again.

When the king's son had eaten and rested a while, he continued on his way again. After a while he came to the same city and the same inn where there was always merriment and never sorrow, and he, too, thought it was a good place to stay; and the first one he met was his brother, and so he stayed there. His brother had feasted and drunk so much that he hardly had any clothes left on his back; but now they began all over again, and there was such dancing and drinking, and pleasure and fun that the second brother also forgot about the bird, and the apple, and his father, and the journey and the whole kingdom. Gone he was and gone he stayed, he too.

When it was getting on for the time that the golden apple would be ripe again, the youngest prince was to go out in the garden and watch for the apple thief. He took with him a friend to help him up in the tree, and a keg of ale and a pack of cards to while away the time and keep them awake. All of a sudden there came a light that shone like a sun, so they could see every feather on the bird while it was still far away. The king's son started climbing up into the tree, and just as the bird snatched the golden apple, he tried to grab it, but all he got was one of its tail feathers. So he went into the chamber where the king lay sleeping, and when he came in with the feather, the room was as bright as the clearest day.

So he, too, wanted to go forth into the wide world to try to find out something about his brothers and capture the bird; for he had been so near that he had left a mark on it and got a feather from its tail, he said. Well, the king pondered a long time as to whether he should let him go, for it wasn't likely that he, who was the youngest, would fare better than the two eldest, who were wiser in the ways of the world, and the king feared that he, too, would be lost. But the youngest son pleaded so earnestly that at last he was allowed to go. So he fitted himself out, and the king equipped him with clothing and money, and then he set off on his way.

When he had travelled a bit, he became hungry and, taking up his knapsack, he sat down to have something to eat; and just as he was doing this, a fox came out from a grove of fir trees, and sat down to watch.

"Oh pray give me a little of your food," said the fox.

"I may well need all I have for myself," said the prince, "for I don't know how far I shall have to travel," he said. "But I have so much that I can at least give you a little."

When the fox had a piece of meat to chew on, he asked the king's son where he was going. Well, that he told him.

"If you will listen to me, I will help you, and luck will be with you," said the fox.

The prince promised, and then they went along together. They travelled for some time until they came to the same city and the inn, where there was always joy and never sorrow.

"I'm afraid I shall have to stay away from here, for the dogs are so troublesome," said the fox, and then he told the prince where his brothers were and what they were doing. "And if you go in there, you will never come any farther," he added.

The prince promised, and gave him his hand on it, that he would not go inside, and then each one went his own way. But when the prince came to the inn and heard the music and merriment, he had to go in, no question about it. And when he met his brothers, there were such carryings on that he forgot about the fox, and the journey, and the golden bird, and his father as well. But when he had been there a while, the fox came — he had ventured into the city after all — and opened the door a crack and winked at the prince, and said that now they must be on their way. So the king's son came to his senses again, and then they set out.

When they had travelled for a while, they saw a huge mountain in the distance, and the fox said, "Three hundred miles beyond that mountain is a gilded linden tree with leaves of gold, and in that linden tree sits the golden bird which the feather comes from."

51

There they travelled together. As the king's son was about to go over and catch the bird, the fox gave him some pretty feathers, which he was to wave and lure the bird down, so it would come flying and perch on his hand. But the fox warned him not to touch the linden tree, for a big Troll owned it, and if he touched even the smallest twig, the Troll would come and kill him on the spot.

No, the king's son certainly would not touch it, he said. But when the bird was perched on his hand, he felt he had to have one twig from the linden tree; he couldn't help himself, it was so bright and fine. So he took just a tiny one. But at the same moment the Troll came out.

"Who's stealing my linden tree and my bird?" roared the Troll, and he was so angry that sparks flew from his eyes.

"A thief thinks that every man steals," said the prince, "but only the one who doesn't steal cleverly enough is hanged!" The Troll said it made no difference, and wanted to kill him. But the king's son pleaded that his life should be spared.

"Well, well," said the Troll, "if you can bring back the horse which my nearest neighbor stole from me, I will spare your life!"

"But where will I find him?" asked the king's son.

"He lives three hundred miles beyond that mountain which is blue on the horizon," said the Troll.

The king's son promised to do his best, but when he came to the fox, *he* was far from pleased.

"Now you have got us in a bad mess," said the fox. "If only you had listened to me, we would have been on our way home by now."

They had to set out on the way again, since it was a matter of life and death and the king's son had promised. And after a while they came to the stable where the prince was to find the horse.

But when he was going in to take the horse, the fox said, "When you get inside the stable, you will see many bridles, both of silver and gold, hanging on the wall. But you must not touch them, for then the Troll will come and slay you on the spot. You must only take the ugliest and most worn-out one you see there."

Well, the king's son promised to do as he was told, but when he got inside the stable, he thought it was downright unreasonable, for there were plenty of fine ones, and so he took the shiniest he could find, and it was as bright as gold. But at that very moment the Troll came out, and he was so angry that the sparks flew.

"Who's stealing my horse and my bridle?" he shrieked.

"A thief thinks that every man steals," said the king's son, "but only the one who doesn't steal cleverly enough is hanged."

"Just the same, I am going to kill you on the spot," said the Troll.

But the king's son thought his life should be spared.

"Well, well," said the Troll, "If you can bring back the lovely maiden my nearest neighbor has stolen from me, I shall spare your life."

All the Trolls burst into a fit of laughter.

"Where does he live, then?" asked the king's son.

"Oh, he lives three hundred miles back of that big mountain which looks blue on the horizon," said the Troll.

Well, the king's son promised to bring back the maiden, and then he was allowed to go, and got away with his life.

But when he came outside, the fox wasn't very happy, you might know. "Now you have got us into a terrible mess again," said the fox. "If only you had listened to me, we could have been on the way home long ago. Now I have a good mind not to stay with you any longer."

But the young prince pleaded so earnestly, and promised to do everything the fox told him to, if only he would stay with him. At last the fox gave in, and they became friends and were on good terms; and so they set out on the way again, and after a while they came to where the lovely maiden was.

"Well," said the fox, "you have promised well enough, but I dare not let you go in to the Troll, all the same. This time I shall go in myself."

So he went in, and after a little while he came out again with the maiden, and then they travelled back the same way they had come.

When they came to the Troll who had the horse, they took both the horse and the shiniest bridle, and when they came to the Troll who had the linden tree and the bird, they took both the linden and the bird and started for home.

When they had travelled for a while, they came to a field of rye. Then the fox said, "I hear a rumbling sound. Now you'll have to travel alone, I am going to stay here for a while." Then he braided himself a garment of rye-straw and put it on, and he looked almost like someone standing there preaching. All at once all three Trolls came rushing up, thinking that they would catch up with them again.

"*Have you seen anyone go by with a lovely maiden, and a horse with a golden bridle, and a golden bird, and a gilded linden tree?*" they shrieked to the fox who stood there preaching.

"Yes, I've heard from my grandmother's grandmother that such a party passed this way. But that was in the good old times when my grandmother's grandmother baked cakes and sold them two for a penny, and gave back the penny into the bargain!"

At this story all the Trolls burst into a fit of laughter: "Ha, ha, ha, ha!" they said, holding onto each other. "If we've been asleep that long, we might as well turn right back and go to sleep again," they said, and then they went back the same way.

The fox set out after the king's son; but when they came to the city with the inn and the brothers, the fox said, "I don't dare go through the city for fear of the dogs. I must go my own way around. But now you must take good care so your brothers don't get hold of you."

But when the king's son came into the city, he thought it would be a shame not to see his brothers and have a few words with them, and so he stopped there a little while. But when the brothers saw him, they came out and took away from him the maiden, and the horse, and the bird, and the linden tree. And they put him in a barrel and threw it into the sea. And then they set off with the maiden, and the horse, and the bird, and the linden tree, and everything, and went home to the king's court.

But the maiden would not talk, and became pale and downhearted; the horse became so thin that it could hardly stand on its legs; the golden bird sat silent and no longer shone; and the linden tree withered away.

In the meantime, the fox prowled about on the outskirts of the city, and waited for the king's son and the lovely maiden, wondering what had become of them. He wandered hither and yon, waiting and longing, and at last came down to the shore; and when he caught sight of the barrel floating on the water, he shouted, "Are you drifting there, you empty barrel?"

"Oh, it's me," said the king's son inside the barrel.

The fox started swimming out in the water as fast as he could go, caught hold of the barrel and dragged it ashore. Then he gnawed at the hoops, and when he had pulled them off the barrel, he said to the king's son, "Kick and stretch!"

The king's son kicked, and pounded and stretched, until each stave gave way, and he hopped out of the barrel. Then they went to the king's court together, and when they arrived, the maiden became beautiful again and started to talk, the horse became so fat and pretty that each hair glistened, the bird shone and sang, and the linden tree bloomed and its leaves sparkled again. And the maiden said, "*There* is the one who saved me."

They put the linden tree in the garden, and the youngest son was to have the princess, for a princess she was. But the two eldest brothers were clapped in spiked barrels and rolled off a steep cliff.

Then they made ready for a wedding. But first the fox begged the king's son to lay him on the chopping block and cut his head off. And for all the king's son tried to get out of it, it was of no avail, he had to do it. But at the very moment he chopped, the fox turned into a handsome prince, and proved to be the brother of the princess they had saved from the Troll. So the wedding was held, and it was so grand and fine, and they celebrated so that people are still talking about it.

THE SQUIRE'S BRIDE

There was once a rich Squire who owned a big manor, and he had silver stored in his chest, and money lent out at interest. But something was wanting, for he was a widower. One day the daughter from the neighboring farm was there working for him. The Squire had taken quite a liking to her, and, as she was the child of poor folk, he thought that if he but hinted at matrimony she would jump at the chance. So he said to her that he had hit upon the idea of marrying again.

"Yes, yes, one can hit upon so many things," said the girl, standing there tittering. She thought the ugly old fellow could have hit upon something which suited him better than getting married.

"Yes, but the idea is that *you* should be my wife!" said the Squire.

Drawings by Erik Werenskiold

The boy threw himself onto the little mare's back, and rode home at full gallop.

She said, "No! Many thanks just the same!" and thought, *that* day will never come.

But the Squire wasn't used to hearing "No!" and the less she wanted him, the more he was bent on getting her. When he could make no headway with the girl, he sent for her father and told him that if he could fix it so he got her, he would forget about the money he had lent him. And he would throw in that piece of land which lay alongside his meadow into the bargain.

Yes, he would soon straighten his daughter out, thought the father. She was only a child and didn't know what was for her own good, he said.

But for all his talking to the daughter, both soft and sharp, it helped not one bit. She wouldn't have the Squire if he sat in powdered gold up to his ears, she said.

The Squire waited day after day, but at last he grew angry and impatient, and so he said to the girl's father that, if he was going to stand by his promise, he had better strike a blow for the cause right away, for he would not wait any longer.

The man knew of no other way, he said, than for the Squire to get everything ready for the wedding. And, when the parson and the wedding guests had come, he was to send for the girl as though there was some work for her to do. And when she came, she must be wedded in a trice before she had time to collect her wits.

This, thought the Squire, was good and well, so he had his servants brew and bake and prepare for the wedding with a vengeance.

When the wedding guests had come, the Squire shouted to one of his boys and said he was to run down to the neighbor south of the farm, and have him send up what he had promised.

"But if you're not back in the twinkling of an eye," he said, shaking his fist, "I'll —" More he didn't get said, for the boy was off as though he had been burnt.

"I'm to greet you from the Master and ask for what you've promised," said the boy to the man south of the farm. "But it has to be this very minute, for he's hopping mad today!"

"Yes, yes! Run down to the meadow and take her with you. She's down there," said the neighbor.

The boy was off. When he came down to the meadow, the daughter was there raking. "I'm to fetch what your father's promised the master," said the boy.

"Aha! They can't fool me that way," she thought. "Oh, is that so?" she said aloud. "It's the little white mare, isn't it? You'll have go to over and take her. She's tethered on the other side of the pea patch," said the girl.

The boy threw himself onto the little mare's back, and rode home at full gallop.

"Did you bring her with you?" said the Squire.

"She's standing out by the door," said the boy.

"Well, lead her up to mother's old room, then!" said the Squire.

"Dear me! How is that to be done?" said the boy.

"You just do as I say!" said the Squire. "If you can't manage her by yourself, you'll have to get folk to help," he said. He thought the girl might get out of hand.

When the boy saw the Squire's face, he realized there was no use arguing out in the yard. So he went down, and took with him all the servants who were there. Some hauled on the front half, and some shoved on the back, and at last they got the mare up the stairs and into the chamber. There lay the bridal outfit ready and waiting.

"Now I've done *that* too, Master," said the boy. "But it was an awful job — the worst I've had here at the farm."

"Well! Well! You won't have done it for nothing," said the Squire. "Now send the womenfolk up to dress her."

Some hauled on the front half, and some shoved on the back, and at last
they got the mare up the stairs and into the chamber.

But when the door opened, and the Squire's Bride came into the great hall,
all the wedding guests burst out laughing.

"But dear me! — After all!" said the boy.

"Don't talk back! They're to dress her up, and they're to forget neither wreath nor crown!" said the Master.

The boy went down in the kitchen.

"Now listen, girls," he said, "you're to go upstairs and dress that little mare as a bride. The Master, no doubt, wants to give the guests a good laugh."

Well, the girls put the bridal outfit on the little mare, and then the boy went down and said she was ready, and wearing both wreath and crown.

"Well done," said the Master. "Bring her down and I'll receive her at the door myself!"

There was a tremendous clattering on the stairs, for she didn't come down in silken shoes, *that* bride. But when the door opened, and the Squire's Bride came into the great hall, all the wedding guests burst out laughing.

And the Squire was so well pleased with that bride, that they say he has never been out courting since!

LITTLE FREDDIE AND HIS FIDDLE

Once there was a peasant who had an only son, and this boy was weak and had poor health so he wasn't able to go to work. His name was Fred, and small he was too, so they called him "Little Freddie".

At home there was little to eat and little to burn, so his father went about the countryside trying to hire him out as a cowherd or errand boy. But he could find no one who would have his boy until he came to the sheriff. The sheriff had just got rid of his errand boy, and there was no one who wanted to go to him as he was known to be a rogue. That was better than nothing, thought the peasant. The boy would at least get something to eat, for at the sheriff's he was to work for his board; and nothing was said about wages or clothing.

But when the boy had been there for three years, he wanted to leave, and then the sheriff gave him all his wages at once. He was to have a penny for each year he had served. "It could not be less," said the sheriff, so the boy got three pennies altogether.

To Little Freddie this seemed like big money, for he had never owned so much before, but still he asked the sheriff if he shouldn't have more.

"You have received more than you should have," said the sheriff.

"Shouldn't I have anything for clothes, then?" said Little Freddie. "The ones I had when I came here are all worn out, and I haven't got any new ones." And now he was so tattered that the rags hung and fluttered on him, he said.

"You have received what we agreed on, and three pennies besides, so I have finished with you," said the sheriff. But the boy was allowed to go out to the kitchen and get a little food in his knapsack; and then he set out on the road to town to buy himself some clothes. He was both happy and merry, for never had he seen a penny before, and from time to time he felt in his pocket to see if he had all three of them.

When he had walked far, and farther than far, he came into a narrow valley with high mountains on all sides, so it didn't seem to him that there was any

Drawings by Th. Kittelsen

way of coming out. He began to wonder what could be on the other side of these mountains, and how he was going to get over them.

He had to go up, so he set out on the way; he wasn't able to go very fast and he had to rest now and then. So he counted his money to see how much he had. When he came up to the very top, there was nothing but a large mossy plateau.

There he sat down and was going to see if he had his money again, but before he knew it, a poor man was standing before him, and he was so big and tall that Little Freddie started to scream when he really saw how big and tall he was.

"Don't be afraid of me," said the poor man. "I'm not going to hurt you. All I ask for is a penny in God's name."

"Mercy!" said the boy. "I only have three pennies, and I was going to town to buy some clothes with them," he said.

"I'm worse off than you are," said the poor man. "I haven't any pennies, and I'm even more ragged than you are."

"Well, then I guess you'll have to have it," said the lad.

When he had gone a bit farther, he became tired and sat down to rest again. When he looked up, another poor man was standing there, but he was even bigger and uglier than the first, and when the boy really saw how big and ugly and tall he was, he started to scream.

"Don't be afraid of me. I'm not going to hurt you. All I ask for is a penny, in God's name," said the poor man.

"Mercy! The truth is," said the boy, "that I have only two pennies, and I was going to town to buy some clothes with them. Had I met you before —"

"I'm worse off than you are," said the poor man. "I have no pennies at all, and a larger body and fewer clothes."

"Well, then I guess you'll have to have it," said the boy.

So he walked a while again until he became tired, and then he sat down to rest, and once he was seated another man was standing before him; but he was so big and ugly and tall that the boy looked upwards and upwards, until he was looking straight up to the sky, and when he really saw how big and ugly and ragged he was, he began to scream.

"Don't be afraid of me, my lad," said the man. "I'm not going to hurt you, for I'm only a poor man who is begging for a penny in God's name."

"Mercy! The truth is," said Little Freddie, "that I have only one penny left, and I'm going to town to buy some clothes with it. If only I had met you before —"

"Well, I have no penny at all, and a bigger body and fewer clothes, so it's worse for me than for you," said the poor man.

Then he would have to have the penny, said Little Freddie. There was no way out of that, for then each one had his and *he* had none.

"Now, since you have been so good-hearted and given away everything you owned," said the poor man, "I will give you a wish for each penny." It

62

"Don't be afraid of me, my lad."

was the same poor man who had received all three pennies. He had just changed his appearance each time so that the boy could not recognize him again.

"I've always loved to hear the fiddle play, and to see people so merry and glad that they danced," said the boy. "So — if I may wish for anything I like — I'll wish for such a fiddle that everything alive must dance to it," he said.

That he should get, but it was a poor wish, said the poor man. "You'll have to wish something better for the other pennies."

"I've always wanted to hunt and shoot," said the boy, "so, if I may wish for what I'd like, then I'll wish me such a musket that I hit whatever I aim at, be it ever so far away."

He should get that, but it was a poor wish, said the poor man. "You'd better wish something better for the last penny."

"I've always longed to be with people who were good and kindhearted," said Little Freddie. "So if I may wish for whatever I'd like, I would want it so that no one could refuse me the first thing I asked for."

"That wasn't such a poor wish," said the poor man, and then he strode away among the hills and was gone. And the boy lay down to sleep, and the next day he came down from the mountain with his fiddle and his musket.

First he went to the storekeeper and asked for clothes; and at one farm he asked for a horse, and at another he asked for a sleigh, and at one place he asked for a fur coat, and not a "No" did he hear, for no matter how stingy they were, they had to give him what he asked for. At last he travelled through the countryside like a real gentleman, with horse and sleigh.

When he had travelled for a while he met the sheriff for whom he had served.

"Good day, master," said Little Freddie, stopping and lifting his cap.

"Good day," said the sheriff. "Have *I* been your master?" he asked.

"Yes, don't you remember that I served you for three years, for three pennies?" said Little Freddie.

"Good gracious! Then you've made good in no time!" said the sheriff. "But how has it happened that you have become such a fine gentleman?"

"Oh, that's a long story," said Little Freddie.

"And are you so bent on pleasure that you travel with a fiddle, too?" said the sheriff.

"Yes, I've always liked to make folk dance," said the boy. "But the finest thing I have is this musket here," he said, "for it brings down everything I aim at, no matter how far away it is. Do you see that magpie sitting in that spruce tree over there?" said Little Freddie. "What will you bet that I can't hit it from where we are now standing?"

The sheriff was willing, if need be, to bet both horse and farm, and a hundred dalers besides, that he couldn't; but as it was, he put up all the money he had with him, and he would fetch the bird when it fell, for he didn't believe that it was possible to shoot so far with any musket. But as soon as the shot was fired, the magpie fell into a big bramble patch, and the sheriff strode all the way in to fetch it, and picked it up. At the same moment Little Freddie started playing his fiddle, and the Sheriff began to dance so the thorns tore at him; and the boy played and the Sheriff danced and cried and pleaded until the rags flew off him, and he had hardly a thread left on his back.

"Well, now I think *you* are just as ragged as *I* was when I left your service," said the boy, "so now I will let you go." But first the sheriff had to pay him what he had bet that the boy couldn't hit the magpie.

When Little Freddie came to town, he went to an inn. He played on his fiddle, and everyone who came there started dancing, and he lived both merrily and well; he had no sorrows for no one could say "No" to what he asked for.

But one day, when the merrymaking was at its liveliest, the watch came to arrest the boy and drag him to the town hall; for the sheriff had complained about him, and said that he had both assaulted and robbed him, and nearly taken his life. And now he should be hanged, there was no way out.

But Little Freddie had a way out of everything, and that was the fiddle. He started to play, and the watch had to dance until they fell down gasping. Then they sent for soldiers and guards, but they fared no better. As soon as Little Freddie took to playing his fiddle, they had to dance as long as he was able to make a sound; but they were worn out long before that.

But finally they sneaked in on him and took him when he was asleep at night, and when they had him, he was sentenced to be hanged right away, and it was off to the gallows at once. A large crowd had come to witness this rare spectacle. And the sheriff was there, too, and he was so overjoyed because he would be repaid for the money and his torn skin, and see that they hanged the boy.

But it didn't go quickly, for Little Freddie was a feeble walker, and he made himself even feebler; the fiddle and the musket he carried along, too, for nobody could get them away from him. And when he came to the gallows, and was going to climb, he rested on every rung of the ladder. On the topmost rung he sat down, and asked if they could refuse him one wish: that he might be allowed to do one thing. He would so like to play just one little tune on his fiddle before they hanged him.

"It would be both a sin and a shame to refuse him that," they said. They couldn't say "No" to what he asked for. But the sheriff begged, in heaven's name, not to let him pluck on a string, or else it would be the end of them all. As for himself, they must *tie* him to the birch tree which stood there, should the boy start playing.

It didn't take Little Freddie long to get the fiddle to sound, and everyone there started to dance, both those on two legs and those on four: both deacon and parson, and clerk and bailiff, and sheriff and hangman, and dogs and pigs. They danced and laughed and shrieked all at the same time; some danced until they lay stretched out as though dead; some danced until they fainted. They all fared pretty badly, but it went worst with the sheriff, for he stood tied to the birch, and danced and rubbed big patches of skin off his back. But

They danced, and laughed, and shrieked all at the same time; some danced until they
lay stretched out as though dead; some danced until they fainted.

no one thought of doing anything to Little Freddie, and he could go wherever
he wished with his fiddle and musket. And he lived happily the rest of his days,
for there was no one who could say "No" to the first thing he asked for.

SORIA MORIA CASTLE

There was once a couple who had a son, and his name was Halvor. From the time he was a small boy he would never do anything, but just sat raking in the ashes. His parents sent him away to learn many different trades, but Halvor would not stick to anything, for when he had been away a few days, he ran away from the trade, came home, and sat down in the hearth and poked in the ashes as before.

Now it happened one day that a skipper came and asked Halvor if he would like to come with him and go to sea, and see foreign parts. Yes, Halvor would like that, and it took him but a short time to get ready.

How long they sailed, I haven't heard, but after a while a terrible storm struck the ship, and when it had abated and the sea was calm again, they didn't know where they were; they had been driven up along a coast unknown to them all.

As it was so still that not even a feather was stirring, Halvor asked the Skipper if he might go ashore and look around, for he would rather walk than lie and sleep.

"Do you think *you* can show yourself to people?" said the Skipper. "Why, you have no other clothes than the rags on your back."

But Halvor insisted, and at last he was allowed to go; but he was to come back as soon as the wind came up. So Halvor went ashore, and it was a lovely land; everywhere he went there were great plains, with fields and meadows, but not a living soul did he see. Then the wind started blowing, but Halvor thought he had not seen enough yet, and he wanted to walk a little longer to see if he could find some people. After a while, he came to a wide road which was so level that one could have rolled an egg on it. On this road Halvor trudged along, and towards evening he saw a great castle in the distance, its windows ablaze with light. He had been walking the whole day, and as he had not had much to eat, he was now quite hungry. But the closer he came to the castle, the more frightened he became.

Inside the castle a fire was burning on the hearth, and Halvor went into the kitchen, which was finer than any kitchen he had ever seen before. The

Drawings by Erik Werenskiold

dishes there were of both gold and silver, but he did not see a living soul anywhere. After he had stood a while, and no one came, he went over and opened a door, and there sat a princess spinning.

"Oh dear me!" she cried. "What Christian soul dares come in here? You had better go again lest the Troll eat you up; for a Troll with three heads lives here!"

"I don't mind if he has four more, I'd like to see that fellow," said the boy. "And I won't leave, because I have done no wrong. But you must give me something to eat, because I am frightfully hungry."

When Halvor had eaten his fill, the princess told him to try to swing the big sword that hung on the wall. But no, he couldn't swing it, he couldn't even lift it once.

"Well," said the princess, "then you must take a swallow from that bottle hanging beside it, for that is what the Troll does when he is going out to use the sword."

Halvor took a swallow, and right away he could swing the sword as though it were nothing. Now, he thought, it didn't matter when the Troll appeared.

All at once the Troll came bursting in; Halvor was behind the door.

"Ugh! Ugh! I smell the smell of Christian blood!" said the Troll, and stuck his head inside the door.

"Yes, and you'll soon know why," said Halvor and chopped off all the heads.

The princess was so happy, now that she had been saved, that she danced and sang, but then she came to think of her sisters, and so she said, "Oh, if only my sisters were saved too!"

"Where are they?" asked Halvor.

Well, she told him: one of them had been taken away by a Troll to a castle six leagues away, and the other was held by a Troll in a castle nine leagues beyond that one. "But first you must help me get rid of this body," she said.

Well, Halvor was so strong, he had the place straightened up and clean in no time. Then he ate, and slept pleasantly and well, and the next morning he started off at dawn, but he knew no peace, and he ran and walked the whole day. When he caught sight of the castle, he became a little frightened again, for it was much finer than the first. But there was not a person to be seen here either; so Halvor went right into the kitchen, and he didn't stop there but went straight on.

"Does any Christian dare come here?" cried the princess. "I don't know how long I have been here, but in all that time I have never seen a Christian soul. You must leave at once, for a Troll with six heads lives here!"

"I wouldn't go," said Halvor, "even if he had six more!"

"He will take and gobble you alive," said the princess.

But that didn't matter. Halvor would not leave, for he was not afraid of the Troll. But he said he would like some food and drink, for he was hungry after the journey.

So he got as much as he wanted, but once again the princess begged him to leave.

"No," said Halvor, "I'm not going, for I have done no wrong, and I haven't anything to be afraid of."

From the time he was a small boy, he would never do anything, but just sat raking in the ashes.

"He won't ask about that," said the princess, "for he will seize you without law or right. But since you won't go, try to swing the sword which the Troll uses to fight with."

He could not swing the sword, but then the princess told him to take a drink from the bottle which hung beside it, and when he had done that he could swing it.

All at once the Troll came, and he was so huge and burly that he had to go sideways to get in through the door. When he had got his first head in, he shouted, "Ugh! Ugh! I smell the smell of Christian blood!"

But right away Halvor chopped off the first head, and then all the others. The princess was so happy that she didn't know which leg to stand on, but then she remembered her sisters, and said that she wished they could be saved too.

Halvor thought it could be managed somehow, and he wanted to be on his way at once. But first he had to help the princess remove the body of the Troll, and the next morning he set out on the way.

It was far to the castle, and he walked and ran to get there in time, but late in the evening he saw it in the distance, and it was even finer than the other two. This time he was not a bit frightened, but went through the kitchen and right in. There sat a princess who was lovelier than any he had ever seen before.

Like her sisters, she told him that there had not been a Christian soul in the place as long as she had been there, and she warned him to leave at once if he wanted to save his life. The Troll would eat him alive — he had nine heads, she said.

"Even if he had nine more, in addition to those nine, and still nine more, I'm not going," said Halvor.

The princess bade him so pitiably to go, but Halvor insisted on staying and said, "Let him come whenever he wants to!"

Then she gave him the Troll's sword, and told him to take a drink from the bottle so he could swing it.

Just then the Troll came rushing in with a great din, and he was even bigger and bulkier than the other two, and he also had to crawl sideways to come through the door.

"Ugh! Ugh! Ugh! Here I smell the blood of a Christian man!" roared the Troll.

At the same moment, Halvor cut off the first head, and then all the others; but the last one was the toughest of them all, and it was the hardest job Halvor had ever had getting *that* off, even though he felt strong enough.

Now all the princesses came together at the castle, and they were happier than they had ever been in all their lives; and they were fond of Halvor, and he was fond of them, and he could have the one he liked best. But of all three, the youngest was fondest of him.

As the days went on, Halvor began to be moody and restless, so the princesses asked what he was brooding over, and if he did not like to be with them. Yes, that he liked, for they had enough to live on, and he was well off in every way. But he was longing for his home, for his parents were still living and he wanted to see them again.

"Ugh! Ugh! Ugh! Here I smell the blood of a Christian man!" roared the Troll.

The princesses told him that it could easily be arranged. "You may go, and you can come back here again, and no harm shall come to you either way if only you do as we now tell you."

Halvor promised to do as they told him, so they dressed him like the finest prince, and put a ring on his finger of such a kind that with it he could wish himself both there and back again. But they warned him not to lose it, and not to mention their names, for then it would be the end of all their happiness, and he would never see them again.

"If only I were home and home were here," said Halvor, and, just as he wished, it came true: he was standing outside his parents' cottage, before he knew it. It was at twilight and when his parents saw this elegant stranger enter, they were quite bewildered, and started to bow and curtsy.

Halvor asked if he could spend the night there.

"Oh, that would be impossible," they said. "We have nothing to offer a fine fellow like you. But go up to the big farmhouse, it's not far, you can see the chimney stack from here. There they have everything."

Halvor did not want to do that, he would rather stay with them. But they insisted he go up to the farm, for there he could get both food and drink, while they had not even a chair to offer him.

"No," said Halvor. "I won't go up there before early tomorrow morning. Let me stay here tonight. Then I can sit by the hearth."

The old people could not refuse him that, so Halvor sat by the hearth and started raking in the ashes, just as he had done when he lived at home.

They talked about many things, and finally Halvor asked if they had ever had any children.

Yes, they had a son, and his name was Halvor, but they didn't know what had become of him, or whether he was dead or alive.

"Couldn't it be me, then?" asked Halvor.

"Oh to be sure!" said the old woman getting up. "Halvor was so lazy, he would never do anything, and his clothes were always in rags and tatters, so he could never have become a fine fellow like you, Sir."

After a while the old woman went over to the hearth to stir up the fire, and as the glow from the embers shone on Halvor's face, she recognized him.

"Well, God bless us! Are you really Halvor?" she cried, and the old parents were quite wild with joy, so happy were they.

He had to tell them everything that had happened to him, and his mother was so fond of him that she wanted to take him up to the big farmhouse at once to show him off to the girls who had always been so proud and haughty.

She led the way, and Halvor went after her. When she got there, she told them that Halvor had returned home, and now they would see for themselves how fine he was. He looks like a prince, she said.

"Oh, a likely story!" said the girls, tossing their heads. "He can't be anything but the ragamuffin he always was."

At that moment Halvor came in, and the girls were so flustered when they

The princesses wanted to sit and rest a bit.

saw him that they left their kirtles by the hearth where they had been sitting and ran out in just their petticoats. When they came back again, they were all so ashamed that they hardly dared look at Halvor, with whom they had always been so grand and haughty before.

"Well, you always thought you were so fine and beautiful that there was no one like you, but you should see the eldest princess I have freed," said Halvor. "Beside her you look like shepherd girls. And the next eldest princess is still more beautiful; but the youngest, who is my sweetheart, is more beautiful than the sun and moon. If only they were here so you could see them for yourself!"

Hardly had he said this, before they stood there. But now Halvor felt so badly, as he remembered what he had promised the princesses. At the farm they had a feast, and a great fuss was made over the princesses. But they would not stay there. "We want to go down to your parents, and look around for a while," they said to Halvor. So he went along.

On their way they came to a large lake, and close by was a lovely green slope where the princesses wanted to sit and rest a bit, and look out over the water. When they had been sitting there for a while, the youngest princess said, "Let me comb your hair for a while, Halvor." Well, Halvor laid his head in her lap, and then she started combing, and it wasn't long before Halvor was asleep.

Then she took her ring off his finger and replaced it with another one, and then she said to her sisters, "Take my hand, as I am taking yours, and let us wish together that we were in Soria Moria Castle."

When Halvor woke up, he realized at once that he had lost the princesses, and he began to wail and lament, and was so disheartened that he could not be consoled. And for all his parents pleaded with him, he would not stay at home, but bade them farewell, saying that he might never see them again, for if he didn't find the princesses again, life would not be worth living.

He had three hundred dalers left, so he put them in his pocket and set out on the way. When he had walked some distance, he met a man with a good horse; he wanted to buy it, so he started bargaining with the man.

"To tell the truth, I hadn't thought of selling it," said the man, "but if we can agree on a price —"

Halvor asked what he wanted for it.

" I didn't pay much for it, nor is it worth much, either. It's a good horse to ride on, but it's not much of a draught horse. It will always carry you and your bag, if you walk a while and ride a while."

At last they agreed on the price, and Halvor put his knapsack on the horse and went on his way, sometimes riding and sometimes walking.

At dusk he came to a green meadow, and there stood a great tree under which he sat down. He let the horse loose to graze, and took his knapsack off the horse. At daybreak he continued on his way, for he could not rest, and was eager to find the princesses. So he walked and rode the whole day, through a deep forest where there were many grassy clearings which shone very prettily through the trees. He did not know where he was nor where he was going, but he took no more time to rest than was needed for the horse to get a little to eat when they came to one of the green spots, and he himself took out his knapsack. He walked and he rode, and thought the forest would never come to an end.

Towards the second evening Halvor saw a light shining through the trees. "If only someone were up, I could warm myself and get something to eat," he thought.

When he came to the light, he saw it was a miserable little hut, and through the window he saw an old man and an old woman inside. Their hair looked like grey moss, and the woman's nose was so long that she sat by the hearth and used it to rake the coals with.

"Good evening," said Halvor.

"Good evening," answered the old woman. "But what is your errand here? Christian folk haven't been here for over a hundred years."

Well, Halvor said that he was on his way to Soria Moria Castle, and asked if she could show him the right way.

"No," said the old woman, "but soon the Moon will come up and I will ask him. He should know, for he shines on everything."

When the Moon rose bright and clear over the treetops, the old woman went outside.

"Oh Moon! Oh Moon!" she shrieked. "Can you tell me the way to Soria Moria Castle?"

"Soon the Moon will come up and I will ask him."

"No, I cannot," said the Moon, "for the time I shone there, a cloud was in the way."

"But just wait a while longer," said the old woman to Halvor. "Soon the West Wind will come by here, and he might know, for he puffs and blows in every direction."

"Well, well, have you a horse too?" asked the old woman when she came in again. "Don't let him stand here by the door and starve. Let the poor creature loose in the field to fill his belly instead! But wouldn't you like to swap it?" she said. "We have a pair of old boots here, in which you can cover a distance of fifteen miles with every step you take. And you can have the boots in exchange for your horse. Then you will be at Soria Moria Castle so much the sooner."

Halvor was quite willing to swap the horse for the boots, and the old woman was so glad to get the horse that she was ready to dance with joy. "For now I can ride to church, I too," she said.

But Halvor was still very restless, and wanted to leave the place at once, but the old woman said there was no hurry. "Lie down on the bench and sleep a little, for we have no bed for you," she said. "I shall keep an eye out for the West Wind when he comes."

All of a sudden the West Wind came roaring so that the walls shook and groaned. The old woman ran outside.

"West Wind! West Wind! Can you tell me the way to Soria Moria Castle? There is someone here who is going there."

"Yes, I know the way very well," said the West Wind. "I am just going to dry some clothes for the wedding which is going to take place there. If he is quick on his feet, he may come along with me."

Halvor rushed out.

"You will have to hurry, if you want to keep up with me," said the West Wind, and he set off over hill and dale, and mountain and valley; and it was all Halvor could do to keep up.

"Well, I have no time to be with you any longer," said the West Wind, "for first I have to blow down a strip of fir trees, before I come to the bleaching place and dry the clothes. But if you will keep to the path running along the edge of the hill, you will come to some girls who are washing clothes, and then you are not far from Soria Moria Castle."

After a while Halvor came to the girls who were washing, and they asked if he had seen anything of the West Wind. He was to come to dry clothes for the wedding.

"Yes," said Halvor, "he is only over knocking down a strip of fir trees. He will be here soon." Then he asked them the way to Soria Moria Castle.

They showed him the road, and when he reached the castle, the court-yard was so full of people and horses that it was swarming. But Halvor's clothes were now so torn and tattered from following the West Wind through bushes and shrubs, that he kept out of sight until dinner time on the day of the wedding.

When, as was the custom, the guests were to drink to the bride, and the master of ceremonies drank with them all, his turn came to drink with Halvor. Halvor drank the toast, then dropped into the glass the ring the princess had placed on his finger when he lay by the water, and bade the master of ceremonies take the glass to the bride and greet her from him. Then the princess got up from the table at once.

"Who deserves best to get one of us," she said, "the one who has freed us, or the groom beside me?"

There was only *one* answer to that, they all felt, and when Halvor heard it, he wasn't long in stepping out of his rags and getting spruced up as a bridegroom.

"Yes, there is the right man!" cried the princess when she caught sight of him.

Then she threw out the other one, and was wedded to Halvor.

76

THE PRINCESS WHO ALWAYS HAD TO HAVE
THE LAST WORD

There was once a king; he had a daughter who was so wayward and willful in her speech that she always had to have the last word, and therefore he promised that the one who could make her hold her tongue should get the princess and half the kingdom into the bargain.

There were plenty who wanted to try, you may believe, for it's not everyday one can get a king's daughter and half a kingdom just for the asking. The gate to the king's manor didn't stop swinging for a moment; they came in flocks and droves, from east and west, both riding and walking. But there was no one who could make the princess stop talking. At last the king made it known that those who tried but couldn't would be branded on both ears with that big branding iron of his — he wouldn't have all this running to his manor for nothing.

Now there were three brothers who had also heard tell of the princess, and, as they weren't well off at home, they wanted to go out and try their luck, and see if they could win the king's daughter and half the kingdom. They were on good terms and got along pretty well, and so they went together, all three.

When they had gone a bit of the way, the youngest brother, who was called the Ash Lad, found a dead magpie.

"Look what I found! Look what I found!" he shouted.

"What've you found?" asked his brothers.

"I found a dead magpie," he said.

"Fie! Drop it! What are you going to do with that?" said the two, who always thought they were the wisest.

"Oh, I've nothing better to do, and nothing better to carry, so I'll just take it along with me," said the Ash Lad.

When they had gone a bit farther, the Ash Lad found an old willow hank, so he picked it up.

"Look what I found! Look what I found!" he shouted.

"What've you found now?" said the brothers.

Drawings by Erik Werenskiold

"I found a willow hank," he replied.

"Pooh! What are you going to do with that? Drop it!" said the two.

"I've nothing better to do, and nothing better to carry, so I'll just take it along with me," said the Ash Lad.

When they had gone a little farther, he found a bit of a broken saucer. This he also picked up.

"Boys! Look what I found! Look what I found!" he said.

"Well, what did you find now?" asked the brothers.

"A bit of broken saucer," he said.

"Ugh! Now *that* was something to take along! Drop it!" they said.

"Oh, I've nothing better to do, and nothing better to carry, so I'll just take it along with me," replied the Ash Lad.

When they had gone a little farther, he found a crooked ram's horn, and just after he found the mate to it.

"Look what I found! Look what I found, boys!" he shouted.

"What've you found *now*?" said the others.

"Two ram's horns," replied the Ash Lad.

"Ugh! Drop them! What are you going to do with them?" they said.

"Oh, I've nothing better to do, and nothing better to carry, so I'll just take them along with me," said the Ash Lad.

In a little while he found a wedge.

"But fellows, look what I found! Look what I found!" he shouted.

"That's a mighty lot of finding you've been doing! What have you found *this* time?" said the two eldest.

"I found a wedge," he replied.

"Oh, drop it! What are you going to do with that?" they said.

"I've nothing better to do, and nothing better to carry, so I'll just take it along with me," said the Ash Lad.

As they walked over the fields by the king's manor — where manure had recently been spread — the Ash Lad bent down and picked up a worn-out shoe sole.

"Say, fellows! Look what I found! Look what I found!" he said.

"If only you'd find a little sense by the time you got there!" said the two. "What did you find this time?"

"A worn-out shoe sole," he replied.

"Ugh! *That* was really something to pick up! Drop it! What are you going to do with it?" said the brothers.

"Oh, I've nothing better to do, and nothing better to carry, so I'll just take it along with me, if I'm to win the princess and half the kingdom," said the Ash Lad.

"Yes, you're likely to do that, you are!" said the two.

Then they were let in to the princess — first the eldest.

"Good day," he said.

"Good day yourself," she said, twisting and turning.

"No, you're not worn-out, but *this* is!" replied the boy.

"It's terribly warm in here," he said.

"It's warmer in the coals," replied the princess. There lay the branding iron, ready and waiting. When he saw that, his courage failed him right away, and so it was all up with him.

The middle brother didn't fare any better.

"Good day," he said.

"Good day yourself," she said, starting to squirm.

"It's terribly hot in here," he said.

"It's hotter in the coals," she said. At that, he too lost both voice and speech, and so it was out with the iron again.

Then came the Ash Lad.

"Good day," he said.

"Good day yourself," she replied, twisting and turning.

"It's good and warm in here," said the Ash Lad.

"It's warmer in the coals," she replied. A third one didn't make her temper any sweeter.

"I suppose I can roast my magpie there, then?" he asked.

"I'm afraid she'll burst," said the king's daughter.

"Oh, that'll be no trouble! I'll put this willow hank around it," replied the boy.

"It's too wide!" she said.

"I'll drive in a wedge!" said the boy, and took out the wedge.

"The fat'll run off her!" said the king's daughter.

"I'll catch it in this!" replied the boy, and held up the bit of broken saucer.

"You're twisting my words!" said the princess.

"No! Your words aren't twisted, but this is!" replied the boy, and took out one of the ram's horns.

"Well! I've never seen the like!" shouted the princess.

"Here's the like of it!" said the boy, and took out the other one.

"You're bent on wearing me out, aren't you?" she said.

"No, you're not worn-out, but *this* is!" replied the boy, and pulled out the shoe sole.

So the princess had to hold her tongue!

"Now you're *mine*!" said the Ash Lad, and so he got her, and half the realm and kingdom into the bargain.

THE ASH LAD WHO HAD AN EATING MATCH
WITH THE TROLL

There was once a farmer who had three sons. He was badly off, and old and feeble, and his sons wouldn't turn their hands to a thing. To the farm belonged a large, good forest, and there the father wanted the boys to chop wood and see about paying off some of the debt.

At last he got them around to his way of thinking, and the eldest was to go out chopping first. When he had made his way into the forest, and had started chopping a shaggy fir tree, a big, burly Troll came up to him.

"If you're chopping in my forest, I'm going to kill you!" said the Troll.

When the boy heard that, he flung aside the axe and headed for home again as best he could. He got home clean out of breath, and told them what had happened to him. But his father said he was chicken-hearted. The Trolls had never scared *him* from chopping wood when he was young, he said.

On the next day the second son was to set out, and he fared just like the first. When he had struck the fir tree a few blows with his axe, the Troll came up to him, too, and said, "If you're chopping in my forest, I'm going to kill you!"

The boy hardly dared look at him. He flung aside the axe and took to his heels just like his brother, and just as fast. When he came home again, his father became angry and said that the Trolls had never scared *him* when he was young.

On the third day the Ash Lad wanted to set out.

"*You?*" said the two eldest. "You'll certainly manage it — you who've never been beyond the front door!"

He didn't say much to *that*, the Ash Lad didn't, but just asked for as big a lunch as possible to take with him. His mother had no curds, so she hung the cauldron over the fire to curdle a little cheese for him. This he put in his knapsack, and set out on his way.

When he had been chopping for a little while, the Troll came to him and said, "If you're chopping in my forest, I'm going to kill you!"

Drawing by Th. Kittelsen

"I'll squeeze you the way I'm squeezing the water out of this white stone!"

But the boy wasn't slow. He ran over to the knapsack to get the cheese, and squeezed it till the whey spurted. "If you don't hold your tongue," he shrieked to the Troll, "I'll squeeze you the way I'm squeezing the water out of this white stone!"

"Nay, dear fellow! Spare me!" said the Troll. "I'll help you to chop!"

Well, on that condition the boy would spare him, and the Troll was clever at chopping, so they managed to fell and cut up many cords of wood during the day.

As evening was drawing nigh, the Troll said, "Now you can come home with me. My house is closer than yours."

Well, the boy went along, and when they came to the Troll's home, *he* was to make up the fire in the hearth, while the boy was to fetch water for the porridge pot. But the two iron buckets were so big and heavy that he couldn't so much as budge them.

So the boy said, "It's not worth taking along these thimbles. I'm going after the whole well, I am!"

"Nay, my dear fellow," said the Troll. "I can't lose my well. *You* make the fire and I'll go after the water."

When he came back with the water, they cooked up a huge pot of porridge.

"If it's all the same to you," said the boy, "let's have an eating match!"

"Oh yes!" replied the Troll, for at *that* he felt he could always hold his own.

Well, they sat down at the table, but the boy stole over and took the knapsack and tied it in front of him, and he scooped more into the knapsack than he ate himself. When the knapsack was full, he took up his knife and ripped a gash in it. The Troll looked at him, but didn't say anything.

When they had eaten a good while longer, the Troll put down his spoon. "Nay! Now I can't manage any more!" he said.

"You *must* eat!" said the boy. "I'm barely half full yet. Do as I did and cut a hole in your stomach, then you can eat as much as you wish!"

"But doesn't that hurt dreadfully?" asked the Troll.

"Oh, nothing to speak of," replied the boy.

So the Troll did as the boy said, and then, you might know, that was the end of him.

But the boy took all the silver and gold to be found in the mountain, and went home with it. With that he could at least pay off some of the debt.

THE COMPANION

There was once a peasant boy who dreamed he was to wed a king's daughter in a far-off land; and she was as red and as white as milk and blood, and so rich that there could never be an end to her riches. When he awoke, it seemed to him that she was still standing before him in the flesh, and he thought her so fine and pretty that he could not live if he did not marry her. So he sold all he owned, and set out into the world to seek her.

He walked far, and farther than far, and in the winter he came to a land where all the highways lay end-to-end in a straight line, and made no turning. When he had wandered straight ahead a three-month's time, he came to a city; and outside the church door stood a big block of ice with a body inside it, and the whole congregation spat on it as they went past.

The boy wondered about this, and when the parson came out of the church, he asked him what it was all about.

"That is a grievous evil-doer," said the parson. "He has been put to death for the sake of his ungodliness, and set up there to be scoffed and scorned."

"What did he do, then?" asked the boy.

"In this life he was a wine-tapper," said the parson, "and he mixed the wine with water!"

That didn't seem to the boy to be such an evil deed, and as long as he had paid for it with his life, they might just as well let him have a Christian burial, and rest in peace after death.

No, said the parson, that could never be, not in any shape or form; for folk were needed to break him out of the ice, money was needed to buy consecrated ground from the church, the gravedigger had to be paid for the grave, the sexton for the hymns, and the parson for the commitment.

"Do you think anyone would pay all that for an executed sinner?" he asked.

Yes, said the boy, once he got him into the ground, *he* certainly would pay for the burial out of the little he had.

Drawings by Erik Werenskiold

"Do you think anyone would pay all that for an executed sinner?" asked the parson.

So they broke the wine-tapper out of the block of ice, and laid him in consecrated ground; they rang and sang over him, and the parson scattered on the earth, and they caroused so at the burial feast that they laughed and cried by turns.

But when the boy had paid for the burial feast, he hadn't many shillings left in his pocket.

He set out on his way again, but he hadn't gone far before a man caught up with him, and asked if he didn't think it was dreary to walk alone.

No, the boy didn't think so, for he always had something to think about, he said.

But maybe he might need a servant all the same, asked the man.

"No," said the boy. "I'm used to being my own servant, and even if I wanted to ever so much, I couldn't afford one, for I haven't money for board and wages."

"You need a servant — I know that better than you," said the man, "and you need a servant you can rely on in life and death. If you won't have me for a servant, you can take me as a companion. I promise that you will benefit by me, and it shan't cost you a shilling. I shall transport myself, and there won't be any need for food and clothing."

Well, on these conditions he'd be glad to have him as a companion.

From then on they travelled together, and most of the time the Companion went ahead and showed the way.

When they had travelled a long way through many a land, over hill and dale, they came to a mountain spur. Here the Companion knocked, and bade whoever was inside to open up. An opening appeared in the rock, and when they had gone a long way inside the mountain, a Troll-hag came forth with a chair and bade them, "Pray sit down, you must be tired," she said.

"Sit down yourself!" said the man.

So she had to sit down, and when she was seated, she remained sitting there, for the chair was such that it did not let go whatever came near it. In the meantime they walked about inside the mountain, and the Companion looked around until he caught sight of a sword hanging over the door. He insisted on having it, and in return he promised the Troll-hag that he would let her out of the chair.

"Nay!" she shrieked. "Ask me for anything else! You can have anything else, but not that, for that's my three-sister-sword!" There were three sisters who owned it together.

"Then you can sit there until the end of the world," said the man.

But when she heard that, she said he could have the sword if only he would let her go.

So he took the sword and left with it, but he left her sitting there just the same.

When they had gone a long way, over bare mountains and broad moors, they came to another mountain spur. There the Companion knocked, and bade whoever was inside to open up. The same thing happened as before: an opening appeared, and when they had gone a long way inside the mountain, a Troll-hag came forth with a chair and bade them sit down; they must be tired, she said.

"Sit down yourself," said the Companion, and then she fared just as her sister. She dared not do otherwise, and when she sat down in the chair, she remained sitting there. In the meantime the boy and the Companion walked about inside the mountain; and the Companion opened all the cupboards and drawers until he found what he was looking for: a ball of golden yarn. He insisted on having it, and he promised the Troll-hag that if she would give it to him, he would let her out of the chair. She said he could have anything else she owned, but *that* she didn't want to lose, for it was her three-sister-ball. But when she heard she would be sitting there until Doomsday if he didn't get it, she said he'd better take it all the same, if only he would let her go. The Companion took it, but he left her sitting where she was.

Then they walked for many days, over moors and through forests, until they came to another mountain spur. There the same thing happened as before: the Companion knocked, an opening appeared, and inside the mountain a Troll-hag came up with a chair and bade them sit down. But the Companion said, "Sit down yourself," and there she sat. They hadn't gone through many of the rooms before he caught sight of an old hat hanging on a peg behind the door. The Companion wanted to have it, but the hag wouldn't part with it, for it was her three-sister-hat, and if she gave *that* away she would be downright unhappy. But when she heard that she would have to remain sitting until the end of the world if he didn't get it, she said he could take it, if only he would let her go. When the Companion had safely got hold of the hat, he left her sitting where she was, just like her sisters.

At long last they came to a fjord. There the Companion took the ball of golden yarn, and threw it so hard against the cliff on the other side of the water that it came back again; and when he had thrown it a few times it became a bridge. They went over the fjord on it, and when they were on the other side, the man bade the boy wind up the yarn again as fast as he could, "for if we don't get it up quickly, the three Troll-hags will come and tear us to bits!" he said. The boy started winding as fast as he could, and when no more than the last thread was left, the Troll-hags came rushing up. They plunged down into the water so the spray rose before them, and made a grab at the end; but they couldn't get hold of it, and so they were drowned in the fjord.

When they had walked some days more, the Companion said, "Now we shall soon come to the castle where she lives — the king's daughter that you've dreamed of. And when we get there, you must go in and tell the king what you've dreamed, and what you're searching for."

When they arrived, the boy did just as he had been told, and he was quite well received; he was given a room to himself, and one for his servant, which they were to stay in, and when it was getting on towards dinner time, he was invited to sit at the king's own table.

When he set eyes on the king's daughter, he recognized her right away, and said that she was the one he had dreamed he was to marry. He told her his errand, and she replied that she liked him well, and would as soon take him.

When no more than the last thread was left, the Troll-hags came rushing up
and made a grab at the end.

But first, she said, he must undergo three trials. When they had eaten, she gave
him a pair of golden scissors, and then she said, "The first trial is that you must
take these scissors and hide them, and give them back to me again tomorrow
at midday. That's not a difficult trial, I hardly think," she said, making a face.
"But if you fail, you'll lose your life, that's the law; and then you'll be executed
and broken on the wheel, and your head placed on a stake, just like those suitors
whose skulls you see outside the windows!" Men's skulls were hanging around
the king's manor like crows sitting on the fence pickets in the fall.

That was easy enough, thought the boy. But the king's daughter was so
frolicsome and wild, and rollicked with him so that he forgot both the scissors
and himself; and while they were romping and disporting themselves, she stole
the scissors from him when he wasn't looking.

When he came up to his chamber in the evening, and related what had happened, and what she had said about the scissors she had given him to hide, the
Companion said, "You do have the scissors she gave you?"

He felt about in his pockets, but no scissors were there, and the boy was
more than beside himself when he realized they were gone.

"Well, well, have patience. I'll have to try to get them back for you again,"
said the Companion, and went down to the stable. There stood a great big ram

which belonged to the king's daughter, and it could fly many times faster through the air than walk on the ground. So he took the three-sister-sword and struck it between its horns and said, "When does the king's daughter ride to her lover tonight?"

The ram bleated and said it dared not say, but when it was struck one more blow, it said that the king's daughter would come at eleven o'clock. The Companion put on the three-sister-hat, which made him invisible, and waited until she came. She smeared the ram with a salve which she had in a great horn, and then she said, "Aloft! Aloft! Over rooftree and church spire, over land, over water, over hill, over dale, to my lover who waits for me in the mountain tonight!"

At the same moment as the ram set off, the Companion flung himself onto its back, and off they went like the wind through the air. They weren't long on the way. All at once they came to a mountain spur. There she knocked, and they passed inside the mountain to the Troll who was her lover.

"Now a new suitor has come to woo me, my friend," said the king's daughter. "He's young and handsome, but I won't have anyone else but you," she said, making herself pleasing to the Mountain Troll. "So I put him to a test, and here are the scissors he was to hide and look after. You take care of them now," she said. Then they both laughed heartily, as though the boy were already being broken on the wheel.

"Yes, I'll hide them, and I'll take care of them! And I'll be sleeping in the arms of the bride, when the raven pecks at the boy's insides!" said the Troll, and put the scissors in an iron casket which had three locks. But at the same moment as he dropped the scissors into the casket, the Companion took them. Neither of them could see him, for he was wearing the three-sister-hat, and so the Troll locked the casket for nothing, and he hid the keys in the hollow tooth where he had a toothache. The boy would have a hard time finding it there, he thought.

When it was getting on past midnight, the princess went home again. The Companion sat on the ram behind her, and they weren't long on the homeward journey.

At dinner time the boy was invited to dine at the king's table, but now the king's daughter made such bored grimaces, and she sat so stiff and straight that she would hardly look in the direction where the boy was sitting.

When they had eaten, she put on her most angelic expression, made herself as sweet as butter, and said, "Perhaps you have the scissors I asked you to hide yesterday?"

"Yes, I have. There they are," said the boy, and he pulled them out and drove them into the table so that plates and dishes jumped. The king's daughter couldn't have been more uncomfortable if he'd hurled the scissors in her face. But she made herself nice and sweet all the same, and said. "Since you've taken such good care of the scissors, it won't be difficult for you to hide my ball of golden yarn, and take care of it so that you can give it back to me by

Then they both laughed heartily.

midday tomorrow. But if you haven't got it, then you'll lose your life and be put to death, for that's the law," she said.

That was an easy matter, thought the boy, and put the ball in his pocket. But she started joking and rollicking with him again, so he forgot both himself and the ball; and while they were romping and disporting themselves to their hearts' content, she stole it from him and let him go.

When he came up to his chamber, and told the Companion what they had said and done, he asked, "You do have the ball of golden yarn which she gave you?"

"Yes, I have it," said the boy and grabbed at the pocket where he had put it. But no, he hadn't any golden ball, and now he was so beside himself again that he didn't know what to do.

"All right, have patience," said the Companion. "I'll have to try to get hold of it," he said, and taking the sword and the hat, he strode off to a blacksmith and had twelve iron crowbars put on his sword.

When he came into the stall, he gave the ram a blow between the horns with the sword, so that the sparks flew, and then he asked, "When does the king's daughter ride to her lover tonight?"

"Twelve o'clock," bleated the ram.

The Companion put on the three-sister-hat again, and waited until she came rushing in with the horn, and smeared the ram. Then she said, like the first time, "Aloft, aloft! Over rooftree and church spire, over land, over water, over hill, over dale, to my lover who waits for me in the mountain tonight!"

Just as they set off, the Companion jumped up onto the ram's back, and they went like the wind through the air. All at once they came to the Troll-mountain, and when she had knocked three times, they flew in to the Troll who was her lover.

"How did you hide the golden scissors I gave you yesterday, my friend?" asked the king's daughter. "My suitor had them and gave them back to me again," she said.

That was downright impossible, said the Troll, for he had locked them in a casket with three locks, and hidden the keys in his hollow tooth. But when they opened it up to look for them, the Troll had no scissors in the casket. Then the king's daughter told him that she had given the suitor her ball of golden thread.

"Here it is," she said, "for I took it from him when he wasn't looking. But what shall we think of now, since he knows such tricks?"

Well, the Troll didn't quite know. But when they had thought about it a bit, they decided to make a big fire and burn the golden ball. Then they'd be certain that he couldn't get hold of it. But at the same moment as she threw the yarn onto the fire, the Companion was ready and grabbed it, and neither of them saw him take it, for he was wearing the three-sister-hat!

When the king's daughter had been with the Troll a while, and it was getting on toward morning, she went home again. The Companion sat on the ram behind her, and they travelled both fast and well.

When the boy was invited to dinner, the Companion gave him the ball. The king's daughter was even more stiff and staid than the last time, and when they had eaten she pursed her lips and said, "I don't suppose it's likely that I'll get back my ball of golden yarn which I gave you yesterday to hide?"

"Why, yes," said the boy. "You shall have it. Here it is!" And he threw it down on the table, so that the table jumped and the king hopped high in the air.

The king's daughter turned as pale as a corpse. But she soon made herself cheerful again, and said that it was well done. Now she had only one more little trial. "If you're clever enough to fetch me what I'm thinking about by midday tomorrow, then I'm yours to have and to hold," she said.

The boy felt as though he had been sentenced to death, for he thought there was no way of knowing what she was thinking about, let alone getting it for her; and when he went up to his chamber, it was almost impossible to calm him. But the Companion told him not to worry. *He* would take care of the matter just as he had done on the other two occasions. And at last the boy calmed down and went to sleep.

In the meantime, the Companion rushed off to the blacksmith and had twenty-four iron crowbars put on his sword. And when that was done, he went to the stall and gave the ram such a blow between the horns that the sound rang around the walls.

"When does the king's daughter go to her lover tonight?" he said.

"One o'clock," bleated the ram.

As the hour approached, the Companion waited in the stall with the three-sister-hat on. And when the princess had smeared the ram and said what she usually said, that they were to fly through the air to her lover who was waiting for her in the mountain, they were off through wind and weather again, with the Companion sitting behind. But this time he wasn't gentle, for all at once he gave the king's daughter a squeeze here and a squeeze there, so hard that he almost crippled her for life. When they came to the mountain spur, she knocked on the gate until it opened, and they flew in through the mountain to her lover.

When she got there, she wailed and carried on, and said that she didn't know the weather could be so rough. But she thought there must have been someone along beating both her and the ram; and indeed she was both black and blue all over her body, so badly had she fared on the way. And then she said that the suitor had found the ball of golden yarn too; how that had happened neither she nor the Troll could understand.

"But do you know what I've hit upon now?" she said.

No, the Troll couldn't know that.

"Well," she replied, "I've told him to get me what I'm thinking about by midday tomorrow, and that was your head. Do you think he can get *that*, my friend?" she said and hugged the Troll.

"I hardly think so!" said the Troll, and he swore to that, and then he laughed and roared, worse than a spirit in torment. And both the king's daughter and the Troll thought that before the boy could get the Troll's head, he would be broken on the wheel, and the ravens would peck out his eyes.

As it was getting on toward morning, she had to go home again. But she was afraid, she said, for she thought there was someone behind her, and she dared not go home alone. The Troll would have to see her home. Yes, he'd go with her, and he got out his ram, for he had one like the king's daughter's, and smeared it well between the horns, too. When the Troll had seated himself, the Companion mounted behind *him*, and off they went through the air, back to the king's manor. But on the way the Companion struck the Troll and the ram, and dealt them blow upon blow with his sword so that they sank lower and lower, and at last they were almost on the point of sinking in the sea they were flying over. When the Troll realized he was so far out of the way, he followed the king's daughter straight back to the king's manor, and waited outside to see that she got home safe and sound. But at the very moment she closed the door behind her, the Companion cut off the Troll's head and strode up to the boy's chamber.

"This is what the king's daughter is thinking about!" he said.

Now, that was both well and good, you might know, and when the boy was invited down to dinner, and had eaten, the king's daughter was as happy as a lark.

"Perhaps you have what I was thinking about?" she said.

"Indeed I have!" said the boy. He pulled it out from under the flap of his robe, and threw it on the table, so that the table and all the things on it were overturned. The king's daughter was as pale as if she had lain in the ground, but she couldn't deny that it was what she had been thinking about, and now he was to have her, as she had promised. So the wedding was celebrated, and there was great joy throughout the whole kingdom.

But the Companion took the boy aside and told him that he could close his eyes and pretend he was asleep on the wedding night, but if he valued his life and would listen to him, he mustn't sleep a wink before he had rid her of the Troll-hide which she was wearing. He was to beat it off her with the twigs of nine new birch brooms, and then rub it off her in three tubs of milk: first he was to scrub her in a tub of last year's whey, and then he was to rub her in sour milk, and then he was to rinse her in a tub of sweet milk. The brooms lay under the bed, and he had put the tubs in the corner. It was all ready. Well, the boy promised he would heed him and do as he said.

When they went to the marriage bed in the evening, the boy pretended to go to sleep. The king's daughter raised herself on her elbows to see if he were asleep, and tickled him under the nose. The boy went on sleeping just as soundly as before. Then she pulled his hair and beard, but he still slept like a log, she thought. Then she took out a big butcher's knife from under the pillow, and was going to hack off his head, but the boy jumped up, knocked the knife out of her hand and grabbed her by the hair. Then he beat her with the broom twigs, and went on thrashing her until there wasn't a stick left. When *that* was done, he threw her in the tub of whey, and then he saw what kind of animal she was: she was as black as a raven all over her body. But when he'd scrubbed her in whey, and rubbed her in sour milk, and rinsed her in sweet milk, the Troll-hide was gone, and she was sweet and pretty as she had never been before.

93

Next day the Companion told him that they had to leave. Well, the boy was ready to travel, and the king's daughter too, for the dowry had long since been ready. During the night, the Companion had carried all the gold and silver and precious things the Troll had left in the mountain to the king's manor, and, when they were about to leave in the morning, the yard was so full that they could hardly get out. The dowry was worth more than the king's land and kingdom itself, and they didn't know how they were to carry it with them. But the Companion knew a way out of all difficulty. There were six of the Troll's rams left, which could fly through the air. These they loaded with so much gold and silver that they had to walk on the ground, and weren't able to raise themselves and fly with it. And what the rams couldn't carry had to remain at the king's court. So they journeyed far, and farther than far, but at last the rams became so tired that they weren't able to go another step. The boy and the king's daughter didn't know what to do, but when the Companion saw that they couldn't move, he put the whole load on his back, placed the rams on top, and carried it so far that there wasn't much more than half a mile left to where the boy had his home.

Then the Companion said, "Now I must leave you. I cannot stay with you any longer."

But the boy didn't want to be parted from him. He didn't want to lose him at any cost. So the Companion stayed with him half a mile more, but he wouldn't come any farther, and although the boy begged and pleaded with him to come home and stay with him, or at least come inside and celebrate the homecoming with his father, the Companion said "No," he couldn't do that.

Then the boy asked what he wanted for having helped him.

If it was to be anything, it must be half of what he bred in five years, said the Companion.

Yes, he would get that.

When he was gone, the boy left all his riches behind and went home empty-handed. Then they celebrated the homecoming until it was both heard of and talked about in seven kingdoms; and when they had finished, it took them the whole winter, using the rams as well as the twelve horses which his father had, to cart all the gold and silver home.

At the end of five years, the Companion came back for his share. Then the boy had divided everything into two equal parts.

"But there's one thing you haven't divided," said the Companion.

"What's that?" said the boy. "I thought I had divided everything."

"You have bred a child," said the Companion. "You must also divide it into two parts."

Yes, that was so. The boy took the sword, but just as he raised it to cleave the child, the Companion grabbed hold of the sword so that he could not strike.

"Weren't you glad that you weren't allowed to strike?" he said.

"Yes, happier than I've ever been," said the boy.

94

Now they must part forever.

"Well, *I* was just as happy when you released me from that block of ice, for I am a wandering spirit," he said.

He was the wine-tapper, who had been frozen fast in the block of ice, on which everyone spat outside the church door. And he had been the boy's Companion and helped him, because he had spent all he had to give him peace and lay him in consecrated ground. He had received permission to serve the boy for a year, and his time had been up when they parted the last time. Then he had been allowed to see him again. But now they must part forever, for the heavenly chimes were calling for him.

BUTTERBALL

There was once an old woman who sat baking. She had a little boy, and he was so round and fat, and fond of good things to eat, that she called him 'Butterball'. And she had a dog called 'Goldtooth'. All at once the dog started to bark.

"Run out, my little Butterball," said the old woman, "and see who Goldtooth's barking at."

So the boy ran out, and came back in and said, "Oh, heaven help me! Here comes a big, tall Troll-hag, with her head under her arm and a sack on her back!"

"Run under the breadboard and hide!" said his mother.

Then in came the big Troll.

"Good day!" she said.

"God bless you!" said Butterball's mother.

"Isn't Butterball at home today?" asked the Troll.

"No, he's in the woods with his father bagging grouse," replied the mother.

"Devil take it!" said the Troll-hag. "I've got such a fine little silver knife I wanted to give 'im!"

Drawings by Th. Kittelsen

"Is Butterball at home today?" asked the Troll.

"Pip, pip! Here I am!" said Butterball, from underneath the breadboard, and out he came.

"I'm so old and my back's so stiff," said the Troll. "You'll have to pop down into the sack and fetch it yourself."

When Butterball was well down inside, the Troll swung the sack on her back and rushed out through the door. But, when they had gone a bit on the way, the Troll grew tired and asked, "How far must I go to find a place to take a nap?"

"A furlong," said Butterball.

So the Troll put the sack down by the side of the road, and went off through the woods by herself, and lay down to sleep.

In the meantime, Butterball saw his chance. He took his knife, ripped a hole in the sack, and popped out. Then he put a large pine root in his place, and home he ran to his mother. When the Troll got home and laid eyes on what she had in the sack, she was beside herself with rage.

The next day the old woman sat baking again. All at once the dog started to bark.

"Run out, my little Butterball," she said, "and see what Goldtooth's barking at."

"Oh nay! Oh nay! That nasty beast!" said Butterball. "Now she's coming back, with her head under her arm and a big sack on her back!"

"Run under the breadboard and hide!" said his mother.

"Good day," said the Troll. "Is Butterball at home today?"

"Indeed he isn't," said the mother. "He's in the woods with his father bagging grouse."

"Devil take it!" said the Troll-hag. "I've got such a pretty little silver fork I wanted to give 'im."

"Pip, pip! Here I am!" said Butterball, and out he came.

"My back's so stiff," said the Troll. "You'll have to pop down into the sack and fetch it yourself."

When Butterball was well down inside the sack, the Troll flung it on her back and set off.

When they had gone a good bit on the way, she grew tired and asked, "How far off is it to where I can sleep?"

"Half a mile," replied Butterball.

So the Troll put the sack down by the side of the road, and went up through the woods, and lay down to sleep. While the Troll was away, Butterball made a hole in the sack, and when he was out he put a big stone inside. When the Troll-hag got home, she made a fire in the hearth, hung a huge pot over, and was going to stew Butterball. But when she took the sack, thinking it was Butterball she was going to shake out, down fell the stone, making a hole in the bottom of the pot, so the water ran out and put out the fire. Now the Troll was terribly angry and said, "No matter how heavy he makes himself this time, I'll trick him just the same, I will!"

The third time was just like the others: Goldtooth started to bark, and so

99

"Now she's coming back, with her head under her arm . . ."

the mother said to Butterball, "Run out, my little Butterball, and see who Goldtooth's barking at."

So Butterball ran out, and came back in again and said, "Oh mercy me! It's that Troll again, with her head under her arm and a sack on her back!"

"Run under the breadboard and hide!" said his mother.

"Good day," said the Troll and stepped in through the door. "Is Butterball at home today?"

"Indeed he isn't!" said the mother. "He's out in the woods with his father bagging grouse."

"Devil take it!" said the Troll-hag. "I've got such a pretty little silver spoon I wanted to give 'im!"

"Pip, pip! Here I am!" said Butterball, and out he came from underneath the breadboard.

"My back's so stiff," said the Troll-hag. "You'll have to pop down into the sack and fetch it yourself."

When Butterball was well down inside, the Troll threw the sack on her back and set off on the way. This time she didn't go off by herself and lie down to sleep, but strode straight home with Butterball in the sack. And when they got there, it was a Sunday.

Then the Troll said to her daughter, "Now you must take Butterball, and cut 'im up, and make broth out of 'im by the time I come back. For now I'm going to church and invite my friends to a feast."

When the Troll had gone, the daughter was going to take Butterball and butcher him, but she didn't quite know how she was to set about it.

"Wait and I'll show you how to go about it, I will," said Butterball. "Lay your head on the stool and you'll see."

She did just so, poor thing, and Butterball took the axe and chopped off her head, just like a chicken's. Then he put the head in the bed and the carcass in the pot, and made broth of the Troll's daughter. And when that was done, he scrambled up over the door, dragging the pine root and the stone with him, and one he placed over the door and the other on the Troll's chimney pipe.

When the folks came home from church and saw the head in the bed, they thought the daughter was asleep; but then they went over to taste the broth.

"Tastes good, this Butterball broth!" said the Troll-hag.

"Tastes good, this daughter broth!" said Butterball, but they paid no attention to that.

Then the Mountain Troll took the spoon and was going to taste.

"Tastes good, this Butterball broth!" he said.

"Tastes good, this daughter broth!" said Butterball, perched up on the chimney pipe.

Then they took to wondering who was talking, and wanted to go out and have a look. But when they got to the door, Butterball threw the pine root and the stone at their heads and killed them all. Then he took all the gold and silver there was in the house — and now he was rich indeed, if you please — and then home he went to his mother.

THE RAM
AND THE PIG
WHO WENT INTO
THE WOODS
TO LIVE
BY THEMSELVES

On a farm there was once a Ram who was being fattened for slaughter, and so he lived well, and grew big and fat from eating all that was good. The dairymaid always came and gave him more.

"Go ahead and eat, Ram," she said, "for you won't be here much longer. Tomorrow we are going to kill you!"

There's an old saying that no one should ever scorn an old woman's advice, for wise counsel and strong drink are given for everything except death itself.

Drawings by Erik Werenskiold

102

"But maybe there's a way out of this too," thought the Ram to himself. So he filled his belly until he could eat no more, butted out the door and dashed over to the neighboring farm and into the pigsty to a Pig, whom he had got to know very well in the field, and since then they had always been friends and on good terms.

"How do you do, and well met again," said the Ram to the Pig.

"How do you do yourself," replied the Pig.

"Do you know why you're so well off, and why they fatten and take such care of you?" said the Ram.

"No, I don't," said the Pig.

"Many thirsty throats soon empty a barrel," said the Ram. "They want to kill you and eat you."

"Is that so?" said the Pig. "I hope they won't forget to say grace before they eat."

"If you would like to do as I would, we can run away to the woods, and build a house and live by ourselves. There's nothing like having your own home, you know," said the Ram.

The Pig agreed and said, "There is happiness in good company."

And so off they went together, and, after they had travelled a while, they met a Goose.

"Hello, good folks. Well met again," said the Goose. "Where are you going in such a hurry?"

"How do you do, and well met yourself," said the Ram. "We were much too well off at home, so now we are going to the woods to live by ourselves; in his own home each man is master."

"Well, I'm pretty well off where I live, myself," said the Goose. "But could I join you? Friendship and play shorten the day, you know."

"With chat and quack one builds neither house nor shack," said the Pig. "So what could you do?"

"Good advice and skill will help a lame man up a hill," said the Goose. "I can pluck moss and stuff the cracks in the walls so that the house would be both warm and snug."

So the Goose was allowed to come along, for the Pig wanted it to be warm and snug. When they had gone a bit farther they met a Hare who came hopping out from the woods.

"How do you do, good folks. Well met again," said the Hare. "How far are you travelling today?"

"Good day, and well met yourself," said the Ram. "At home we were much too well off, but now we are going into the woods to build a home for ourselves. When the temptation is gone, home is best!"

"Well, I have my home under every bush in the woods," said the Hare. "But when winter comes, I often say to myself that if I live until next summer, I shall build a real house for myself. So I would almost like to come along and build one at last."

"If we were molested on our way, you could not keep the hounds at bay!" said the Pig. "Besides you wouldn't be of much use to us in building a house."

103

"For everyone living there is taking and giving," said the Hare. "I have sharp teeth to shape wooden pegs with. And with my paws I can hammer them into the wall, so I will always be a good carpenter, for it takes good tools to do good work, as the man said when he skinned his mare with an auger."

So the Hare, too, was allowed to come along, and they all went on together.

When they had trudged along for a while, they met a Cock.

"Good day! Good day, good folks, and well met again!" said the Cock. "And where are you bound for today?"

"Good day to you, too, and well met yourself," said the Ram. "At home we were much too well off. So now we are going into the woods to build a house and live by ourselves. For the one who goes out to bake loses both coal and cake," he said.

"Well, I am pretty well off where I am," said the Cock. "But better to build your own place anywhere than sit on another's perch and gape and stare. A cock should always be his own master. So, if I could join such fine company, I would like to come along and build a house!"

"All your cackling and crowing will help to keep the axes going, but your morning laughter won't help raise the rafter. So you can't help us build a house," they said.

"A place without a dog or a cock is like a house without a clock," said the Cock. "I am early awake and early to wake."

"Yes, early awake more gold you make, so let him come along too," said the Pig, who was a terrible sleepyhead. "Sleep is a great thief; he will always steal half the time."

So they all trudged along to the woods, one after the other, and built the house. The Pig hewed the timber, and the Ram carried it home. The Hare was the carpenter, gnawing pegs and hammering them into walls and roof. The Goose picked moss and stuffed it into the cracks. And the Cock crowed and took care that no one overslept in the morning.

When the house was finished and the roof covered with bark and turf, they all lived happily by themselves and fared good and well.

But a little farther over in the woods was a lair in which two Wolves were living. When they saw that a new house had sprung up in their neighborhood, they wanted to find out what kind of folks their neighbors might be, for a good neighbor is better than a brother in a far off land, and it is better to live in a friendly neighborhood than to be widely known.

So one of them feigned an errand, and went in and wanted to borrow a light for his pipe. But as soon as he came in through the door, the Ram butted him so hard that he fell headlong into the fireplace. The Pig started beating and biting, the Goose started hissing and nipping, the Cock started crowing and yelling at the top of his lungs, but the Hare was so scared out of his wits that he ran high and low and tramped and trod in every corner.

At last the Wolf came out again.

"But if *he* had caught me, I never would have come out alive!"

"I suppose you found that good neighbors make good friends," said the Wolf who had waited outside. "You must have found it a paradise on earth since you stayed so long. But how did it go with the light? Why, you have neither smoke nor pipe!" he said.

"Well, that was a strange light and a strange company," said the Wolf who had been inside. "Such folks and such manners I have never seen before; but as one chooses his company so is one rewarded, and unexpected guests might not always be welcome," said he. "When I came inside the house, the shoemaker threw a sack at me, so I tumbled headlong into the smithy; there sat two smiths blowing their bellows, and they tore bits of flesh from my body with red-hot tongs and pincers! The hunter ran about like a madman looking for his gun, and it was just luck that he did not find it, and a fellow who sat perched high under the ceiling flapped and shouted: 'Put the hook in 'im and drag 'im here! Drag 'im here!' But if *he* had caught me, I never would have come out alive!"

THE FOX AS SHEPHERD

Once upon a time there was a woman who was going out to hire a shepherd. Then she met a bear.

"Where are you going?" said the bear.

"Oh, I'm going to hire myself a shepherd," answered the woman.

"Won't you have me for your shepherd?" asked the bear.

"Yes, if only you know how to call the animals," said the woman.

"Brrrrr," growled the bear.

"No, you won't do!" said the woman, when she heard that, and went on her way.

After walking along for some time she met a wolf.

"Where are you going?" said the wolf.

"I'm going to hire myself a shepherd," said the woman.

"Could I be your shepherd?" asked the wolf.

"Well, if only you know how to call the animals," said the woman.

"Ouh, ouh, ouh!" said the wolf.

Drawings by Erik Werenskiold

"Oh no! I don't want you," she said.

When she had gone a little farther, she met a fox.

"Where are you going?" asked the fox.

"Oh, I'm looking for a shepherd to hire," said the woman.

"Will you hire me as your shepherd?" said the fox.

"Yes, if you know how to call the animals," the woman said.

"Dilly, dally, holli, dolli," cried the fox in a clear and ringing voice.

"Yes, you're just the right fellow I want for a shepherd," said the woman, and hired the fox on the spot.

The first day the fox was to herd the livestock, he ate up all the woman's goats. The next day he gobbled up all her sheep, and on the third day he ate up all her cows.

When he came home in the evening, the woman asked what he had done with all her animals, as she could see none around.

"Their skulls are in the river and their bones are in the woods," said the fox.

The woman was busy churning butter, but she thought she had better go outside to see what had become of all her animals, and while she was gone, the fox popped down in the churn and ate up the cream. When the woman came back and saw what the fox had done, she was so angry that she took the little drop of cream that was left and threw it at the fox, so he got a drop on the tip of his tail.

And that is why the fox has a white tip on his tail to this very day.

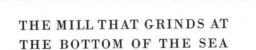

THE MILL THAT GRINDS AT
THE BOTTOM OF THE SEA

Once, in the old, old days, there were two
brothers; one was rich and the other was poor.
When it was Christmas Eve, the poor brother
hadn't a crumb of food in the house — neither
clabber nor bread—and so he went to his brother and begged for a little food for Christmas.
It certainly wasn't the first time the brother had
had to give him something; but *he* was always
stingy, and he didn't grow any fonder of him
this time, either.

"If you'll do what I ask you, you'll get a
whole ham," he said. The poor wretch promised
on the spot, and thanked him into the bargain.

"There it is. Now go straight to the Devil!"
said the rich one, and flung the ham at him.

"Well, whatever promise I've made I'll have
to keep," said the other. He took the ham and
set out on the way.

Drawings by Erik Werenskiold

He walked and he walked the whole day, and at nightfall he came to a place all splendidly lighted up. "This is the place," thought the man with the ham. Out in the woodshed stood an old man with a long white beard, chopping wood for Christmas.

"Good evening!" said the man with the ham.

"Good evening, yourself! Where are you off to so late?" said the old fellow.

"Why, I'm going to the Devil, if I'm on the right road," replied the poor man.

"Oh, you've gone right enough, for here you are," said the other. "Now when you go inside, they'll all want to buy your ham, for it's uncommon fare here. But you're not to sell it unless you get the handmill, which stands behind the door, for it. Then, when you come out again, I'll teach you how to stop the mill. It's good for a little of everything, that mill is."

Well, the man with the ham thanked him for his good advice, and knocked at the Devil's door.

When he went in, everything happened just as the old man had said: all the devils, both big and small, swarmed around him like ants, and each one outbid the other for the ham.

"To be sure, my old woman and I were going to have it for our Christmas dinner, but since you're so bent on having it, I dare say I'll just have to leave it with you," said the man. "But if I'm going to sell it, I want the handmill behind the door over there."

The Devil was loath to part with the mill, and he haggled and bargained, but the man held out, and at last the Devil had to hand it over.

When the man came out into the yard, he asked the old woodcutter how to stop the mill, and when he had learned that, he said his thanks and set out for home as fast as he could; but still he didn't reach home before the clock struck twelve on Christmas Eve.

"Where in the world have you been, then?" said the old woman. "Here I've been sitting hour in and hour out, waiting and yearning, without so much as two sticks to lay in a cross under the pot of Christmas porridge!"

"Oh, I couldn't get here any sooner. I had a little of everything to fetch, and the way was long, too. But now you'll see!" He put the mill on the table and bade it first grind out candles, then a cloth, and then food and ale, and all that was good for Christmas fare. And, according to what he said, the mill ground.

The old woman crossed herself again and again, and wanted to know where the man had got the mill from, but he wouldn't tell that.

"It makes no difference where I got it. You see the mill is good, and the millstream doesn't freeze over," said the man. Then he went on grinding out food and drink, and all kinds of good things for Christmas, and on the third day he invited his friends to come, for now he wanted to have a feast.

When the rich brother saw all the things there were at the feast, he became wild with rage, for he begrudged his brother everything.

"On Christmas Eve he was so poverty-stricken that he came to me and begged for a little in God's name. And now he's giving a party as if he were both count and king," he said.

"But where in the devil did you get all your riches from?" he said to the brother. "Behind the door," said the man who owned the mill. *He* certainly wasn't going to account to his brother for that. But later in the evening, when a little ale had gone to his head, he couldn't help himself, and he brought out the mill. "There you see what's brought me all my riches!" he said, and he had the mill grind out one thing after another. When the rich brother saw that, he wanted to have the mill at any cost, and at last he got it, too. But he had to give three hundred *dalers* for it, and the other was to keep it until haying time. "For if I have it that long, I can grind out food for many a year," he thought. In the interval you can be sure the mill didn't grow rusty, and when haying time came, the rich brother got it. But the other had taken good care not to teach him how to stop it.

It was evening when the rich brother took the mill home, and the next morning he bade his wife go out and spread hay after the mowers. He would make lunch himself today, he said.

When it was getting on toward lunch time, he put the mill on the kitchen table. "Grind out herring and porridge, and do it both fast and well!" said the man. The mill started to grind out herring and porridge, first all the dishes and troughs full, and then all over the kitchen floor. The man fumbled with the mill, and tried to get it to stop, but for all he turned and prodded it, the mill kept on grinding, and in a little while the porridge reached so high that the man was close to drowning. So he threw open the parlor door, but it wasn't long before the mill had ground the parlor full, too, and it was only in the nick of time that the man got hold of the doorknob down in the flood of porridge. It's safe to say he didn't stay long in the parlor once he got the door open. He rushed out, with herring and porridge pouring out after him over both yard and fields.

Now the old woman, who was busy spreading hay, began to think that time was dragging on too long before lunch was ready. "If my man doesn't call us home, we'll have to go all the same. He certainly doesn't know much about cooking porridge. I'll just have to help him," said the wife to the mowers.

So they headed for home. But when they had gone a little way up over the hill, they met herring and porridge and bread, rushing and pouring pell-mell, and the man, himself, leading the flood.

"If only there were a hundred bellies to each of you! But take care you don't drown in the porridge!" he cried, and lit out past them as though the Devil himself were at his heels, down to where the brother lived. He begged him, for goodness sake, to take back the mill that very minute. "If it grinds one more hour, the whole parish will drown in herring and porridge!" he said. But the brother wouldn't take it unless the other one paid him three hundred *dalers* more. So he had to pay.

Now the poor brother had both money and mill, and it wasn't long before he put up a manor for himself much finer than the one the brother lived in. With the mill he ground out so much gold that he covered the manor only with sheets of gold, and that manor stood close to the shore, so it shone and sparkled far out over the fjord. Now everyone who sailed past there wanted to drop in and pay his respects to the rich man in the golden manor, and they all wanted

He rushed out, with herring and porridge pouring out after him over both yard and fields.

to see that wonderful mill, for word of it had spread far and wide, and there was no one who had not heard of it.

After a long time there also came a skipper who wanted to see the mill; he asked if it could grind out salt. Why yes, it could grind out salt, said the owner. When the skipper heard that, he determined to get the mill by force if need be, cost what it might; for if he had it, he thought, he'd get out of having to sail far away over sea and foam after cargoes of salt. At first the man wouldn't part with the mill, but the skipper begged and pleaded, and at last he sold it and got many, many thousands of *dalers* for it, too.

When the skipper had put the mill on his back, he didn't stay there long for fear the man would change his mind; he had no time at all to ask how to stop the mill, but headed down to the ship as fast as he was able. And, when he had sailed a little distance out to sea, he brought the mill up on deck.

"Grind salt, and do it both fast and well!" said the skipper. Well, the mill started grinding salt so fast that it spouted. When the skipper had the ship full, he wanted to stop the mill; but no matter what he did, or how he handled it, the mill went on grinding just as fast as ever, and the pile of salt grew higher and higher, until at last the ship went down.

And there sits the mill at the bottom of the sea, grinding away to this very day. And *that* is why the sea is salt!

THE OLD WOMAN AGAINST THE STREAM

There was once a man who had an old wife, and she was so cross and contrary that she was hard to get along with. The man, in fact, didn't get along with her at all. Whatever *he* wanted, she always wanted the very opposite.

Now one Sunday in late summer it happened that the man and the wife went out to see how the crop was getting along. When they came to a field on the other side of the river, the man said, "Well, now it's ripe. Tomorrow we'll have to start reaping."

"Yes, tomorrow we can start to clip it," said the old woman.

Drawings by Erik Werenskiold

Then the man flew into a rage, and ducked her both good and long.

"What's that? Shall we clip? Aren't we going to be allowed to reap either, now?" said the man.

No, clip it they should, the old woman insisted.

"There's nothing worse than knowing too little," said the man, "but this time you certainly must have lost what little wits you had. Have you ever seen anyone *clip* the crop?"

"Little do I know, and little do I care to know," said the old woman, "but this I know to be sure: the crop is going to be clipped and not reaped!" There was nothing more to be said. Clip it they should, and that was that.

So they walked back, wrangling and quarreling, until they came to a bridge over the river, just by a deep pool.

"It's an old saying," said the man, "that good tools do good work. But I dare say *that'll* be a queer harvest which they clip with sheepshears!" he said. "Shan't we be allowed to reap the crop at all, now?"

"Nay, nay! — Clip, clip, clip!" shrieked the old woman, hopping up and down, and snipping at the man's nose with her fingers. But in her fury she didn't look where she was going, and she tripped over the end of a post in the bridge and tumbled into the river.

"Old ways are hard to mend," thought the man, "but it'd be nice if I were right for once — me too."

He waded out in the pool and caught hold of the old woman's topknot, just when her head was barely above the water. "Well, are we going to reap the field?" he said.

"Clip, clip, clip!" shrieked the old woman.

"I'll teach you to clip, I will," thought the man, and ducked her under. But it didn't help. They were going to clip, she said, when he let her up again.

"I can only believe that the old woman is mad!" said the man to himself. "Many people are mad and don't know it; many have sense and don't show it. But now I'll have to try once more, all the same," he said. But hardly had he pushed her under before she thrust her hand up out of the water, and started clipping with her fingers as with a pair of scissors.

Then the man flew into a rage, and ducked her both good and long. But all at once her hand sank down below the surface of the water, and the old woman suddenly became so heavy that he had to let go his hold.

"If you want to drag me down into the pool with you now, you can just lie there, you Troll!" said the man. And so there the old woman stayed.

But after a little while, the man thought it a pity that she should lie there and not have a Christian burial. So he went down along the river, and started looking and searching for her. But for all he looked and for all he searched, he couldn't find her. He took with him folk from the farm, and other folk from the neighborhood, and they all started digging and dragging down along the whole river. But for all they looked, no old woman did they find.

"No," said the man. "That's no use at all. This old woman had a mind of her own," he said. "She was so contrary while she was alive that she can't very well be otherwise now. We'll have to start searching upstream, and try above the falls. Maybe she's floated herself upstream."

Well, they went upstream, and looked and searched above the falls. There lay the old woman!

She was *the old woman against the stream*, she was!

THE HARE WHO HAD BEEN MARRIED

There was once a Hare who went for a walk in the green field. "Hop and skip and jump ahigh," sang the Hare in great glee, and bounced and vaulted hither and thither, and now and then he stood up on his hind legs and looked around and listened.

Then a Fox came sneaking across the field.

"Good day, good day," said the Hare. "I'm so happy today for having been married, so happy that I must tell you all about it."

"That must have been very nice," said the Fox.

"Well, it wasn't always so nice either, for she was pretty tough at times too. A real devil she could be, the one I got for a wife," said the Hare.

"It must have been really too bad for you, then," said the Fox.

"Oh, but it wasn't altogether as bad as it might have been. I got a good dowry with her, for she had a house of her own," said the Hare.

"But that was a fine thing to get," said the Fox.

"Well, that wasn't so good either, for the house burnt down," said the Hare. "And everything we owned went up in flames."

"Oh, but that really *was* too bad!" said the Fox.

"No, it wasn't so bad after all, for she burnt up with it," said the Hare.

Drawing by Erik Werenskiold

THE HOUSE MOUSE
AND THE COUNTRY MOUSE

There were once a House Mouse and a Country Mouse who met on the edge of the forest. The Country Mouse sat in a hazel bush gathering nuts.

"Blessings on your work!" said the House Mouse. "Do I meet kinsfolk so far out here in the country?"

"Yes, indeed," said the Country Mouse.

"You're gathering nuts, I see, and taking them home," said the House Mouse.

"I have to, if we're to have anything to live on during the winter," said the Country Mouse.

"The husks are big and the shells are full this year, so they'll go a long way to fill stomachs," said the House Mouse.

"That is indeed so," said the Country Mouse, who declared that she was well off and lived comfortably.

The House Mouse maintained that she was better off; but the Country Mouse stuck to her point, and said there was no place as good as forest and mountain, and that she was better off herself. The House Mouse said *she* was better off, and this they could not agree on. At last they promised to visit one another at Christmas time so they could see which one was better off.

The House Mouse was the first to go on her Christmas visit. She scurried through forest and deep valleys, and even though the Country Mouse had moved down the mountain for the winter, the way was both long and hard. It was uphill, and the snow was deep and loose, so that she grew both tired and hungry before she got there.

"Now it will be good to have some food," she thought when she arrived.

The Country Mouse had scraped together pretty well: there were nut kernels, and many different kinds of roots, and all sorts of good things which grow in

Drawings by Th. Kittelsen

116

forest and field. She had stored it all in a hole deep down in the ground so that it wouldn't freeze. Close by was a spring which was open the whole winter so she could drink as much water as she wanted.

There was enough of what there was, and they ate both heartily and well; but the House Mouse thought it no more than the bare necessities of life.

"On this one can keep alive," she said, "but it's not particularly good. Now you must be so kind as to come to see me, and taste my food."

Yes, this the Country Mouse would do, and it wasn't long before she came. The House Mouse had gathered together all the Christmas fare which the wife of the house had spilled. There were bits of cheese, and butter, and tallow, and crumbs of buttered bannock and oatcakes spread with cream. In the pan set to catch the drip from the beer tap she had drink enough, and the whole parlor was filled with all kinds of good things to eat. They ate and lived well, and there was almost no end to the Country Mouse's appetite: such food she had never tasted. Then she became thirsty, for the food was both rich and fat, she said, and at last she had to have a drink.

"It's not far to the beer. This is where we drink," said the House Mouse, and she jumped up on the edge of the pan; but she drank no more than would quench her thirst for she knew the Christmas beer and knew it was strong. But the Country Mouse thought it was a glorious drink — she had never tasted anything but water — and took one sip after the other. She wasn't used to

Then she became light-headed, and it went to her feet, and she took to running and hopping from one beer barrel to the other.

And whoosh! The Country Mouse darted into the hole of the House Mouse.

strong drink, so she was tipsy before she came down off the pan. Then she became light-headed, and it went to her feet, and she took to running and hopping from one beer barrel to the other, and dancing and cavorting on the shelves among the cups and mugs, and peeping and squeaking as though she were both drunk and mad — and drunk she was, too, by now!

"You mustn't carry on as though you've just come out of the mountain today," said the House Mouse. "Don't make such a fuss and don't kick up such a racket. We've got quite a strict bailiff here," she said.

The Country Mouse said she respected neither bailiff nor tramp.

But the Cat sat dozing on the cellar door, and heard both the chattering and the commotion. Just then the wife went down to tap beer into a jug, and lifted up the door, so the Cat slipped into the cellar and pounced on the Country Mouse. And now she danced to another tune, I can tell you. The House Mouse popped into her hole, and sat safely watching the Country Mouse, who sobered up at once when she felt the Cat's claws.

"Oh, my dear bailiff! My dear bailiff! Have mercy and spare my life, and I'll tell you a story," she said.

"Out with it!" said the Cat.

"Once there were two little mice," said the Country Mouse, squeaking slowly and so pitiably, for she wanted to drag it out as long as she could.

"Then they weren't alone!" said the Cat, both short and cross.

"Then we had a roast we were going to roast for ourselves."

"Then you didn't go hungry!" said the Cat.

"Then we put it out on the roof to cool off," said the Country Mouse.

"Then you didn't burn yourselves," said the Cat.

"Then the Fox and the Crow came and took it and ate it," said the Country Mouse.

"Then I'm going to eat you!" said the Cat.

But at that moment the wife slammed the cellar door, and the Cat was so startled that he let go his hold. And whoosh! The Country Mouse darted into the hole of the House Mouse. From there she went right out into the snow, and she wasn't slow in heading for home.

"You call this being well off, and say that you live best?" the Country Mouse said to the House Mouse. "Heaven content me with less, then, instead of such a big manor and such a hawk for a bailiff. Why, I barely got away with my life!"

THE BEAR AND THE FOX WHO MADE A BET

There was once a Bear who came trudging across a swamp carrying a fat pig. The Fox sat high up on a stone by the edge of the swamp.

"How do you do, grandpa," said the Fox. "What is that good thing you have there?" he asked.

"Pork!" said the Bear.

"I, too, have something that tastes very good," said the Fox.

"What's that?" said the Bear.

"It's the largest bees' nest I've ever found," said the Fox.

"Is that so?" said the Bear, grinning and drooling. How good he thought it would be to have a little honey!

"Shall we swap?" said the Bear.

"Oh no! Not me!" said the Fox.

But then they made a bet, and agreed that they were to name three different kinds of trees. If the Fox could say it faster than the Bear, he should get one bite of the pork. But if the Bear could say it faster, he was to have one suck at the nest. He would certainly manage to drain all the honey in one suck, thought the Bear.

"That will be all right with me," said the Fox. "But if I win, I want you to pull out all the bristles where I want to bite."

"To be sure. I'll do it if you can't manage it yourself," said the Bear.

So then they got ready to name the trees.

Drawings by Th. Kittelsen

120

"*Spruce, fir* and *pine!*" growled the Bear in a gruff voice.

But this was only one tree, for spruce is nothing but fir.

"*Ash, aspen, oak!*" shrieked the Fox so the forest rang.

Now he had won the bet, and he rushed down and took the heart out of the pig in one bite, and was about to run away. But now the Bear was angry because the Fox had taken the choicest part of the whole pig, and, catching the Fox on the run, he held him fast by his tail.

"Wait a bit!" shouted the Bear and was white with rage.

"Well, it's the same to me, grandpa. If you'll let me go, I'll give you a taste of my honey," said the Fox.

When the Bear heard that, he let go his hold, and the Fox went up after the honey.

"Here on this bees' nest," said the Fox, "I'm holding a leaf, and under that leaf is a hole which you can suck through," he said. And at the same moment as he held the nest up under the Bear's nose, he took the leaf away, hopped up on the stone, and began to giggle and laugh. For there was neither a bees' nest nor honey. It was a wasps' nest as big as a man's head, full of wasps; and the wasps came swarming out of the nest and stung the Bear's eyes and ears and mouth and nose. And he was so busy scraping them off that he had no time to think of the Fox.

From that day all bears have been afraid of wasps.

SQUIRE PER

There was once a poor couple; they had nothing but three sons. What the two eldest were called, I do not know, but the youngest was named Per.

When the parents died the children were to inherit from them, but there was nothing left but a pot, a griddle and a cat. The eldest, who was to have first choice, took the pot. "When I loan out the pot, I'll always be allowed to scrape it," he said. The next one took the griddle. "For when I loan out the griddle, I'll always get a taste of oatcake," he said. But the youngest had no choice; if he wanted anything, it would have to be the cat. "If I loan out the cat, then I won't get anything for her, I'm sure," he said. "If the cat gets a drop of milk, she'll have it herself. But I'd better take her along all the same. It would be a shame for her to wander about here and die."

Drawings by Erik Werenskiold.

So the brothers set out into the world to seek their fortunes, and each took his own way.

But when the youngest had walked a while, the cat said, "You shall indeed be repaid for not wanting to leave me behind in that old cottage to die. Now I'm going into the forest to find some strange animals. Then you're to go up to the king's manor you see over there, and say you have come with a little present for the king. And when he asks who it's from, you're to say it's from 'Squire Per'."

Well, Per hadn't waited long before the cat came back with a reindeer from the forest. She had jumped up onto the reindeer's head, and sat down between its horns. "If you don't go straight to the king's manor, I'll scratch out your eyes!" she said, and then the reindeer dared not do otherwise.

Now when Per came to the king's manor, he went into the kitchen with the reindeer and said, "I've come with a little present for the king, I have, if he won't look down his nose at it."

The king came out to the kitchen, and when he saw that fine reindeer he certainly was glad. "But my dear friend, who is sending me such a generous gift?" said the king.

"Oh, it comes from Squire Per, to be sure," said the boy.

"Squire Per?" said the king. "Now where would *he* be living?" he said, for he thought it a shame not to know such a fine man.

But the boy wouldn't tell that at all; he dared not for fear of his master, he said. So the king gave Per a big tip, and bade him greet them heartily at home, and say many thanks for the present.

The next day the cat went to the forest again, and jumped onto the head of a stag, sat herself between its eyes, and forced it to go to the king's manor. There Per went with it into the kitchen again, and said he had come back with a little present for the king, if he wouldn't look down his nose at it. The king was even happier about the stag than he had been about the reindeer, and asked again who could be sending him such a generous present.

"It's from Squire Per, to be sure," said the boy, but when the king wanted to know where Squire Per lived, he got the same answer as the day before, and that time Per received an even bigger tip.

On the third day the cat came with an elk. So when Per went into the kitchen of the king's manor, he said that he had still another little present for the king, if he wouldn't look down his nose at it. The king came out to the kitchen at once, and when he caught sight of that big, fine elk, he was so happy that he didn't know which foot to stand on, and that day he gave Per a much, much bigger tip; indeed, it was a hundred *dalers*. He insisted on knowing where Squire Per lived, and pried and asked questions about one thing and another; but the boy said that he dared not tell because his master had forbidden it, and that both strictly and sternly.

"Then bid Squire Per to look in on me," said the king.

Yes, that would do, the boy said.

123

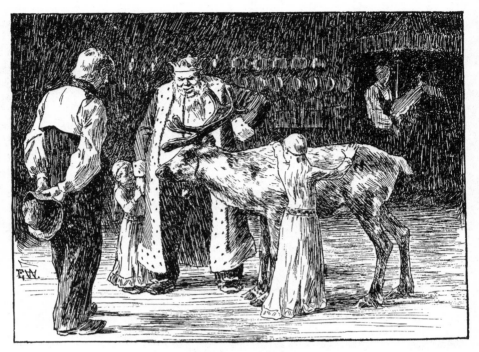

"Squire Per?" said the king.

But when he came out of the king's manor again, and met the cat, he said, "Well, you've landed me in a fine mess, you have. Now the king wants me to pay him a visit, and I have nothing but these rags I stand and walk in."

"Oh, don't be afraid about that," said the cat. "In three days you shall have horses and a carriage, and such fine clothes that the gold will be dripping off you. Then you can certainly visit the king. But no matter what you see at the king's manor, you're to say that everything is much finer and more splendid at home. That you must not forget!"

No, Per certainly wouldn't forget that, he thought.

When the three days were up, the cat came with a carriage and horses, and clothing, and all that Per needed; everything was so fine that no one had seen such things before. Then he set out, and the cat sprang along ahead. The king received him both kindly and well, but no matter what the king offered him, and no matter what he showed him, Per said it was good enough, but what he had at home was even finer and more splendid. The king didn't like this at all, but Per stuck to it, and at last the king grew so angry that he couldn't control himself any longer.

"Now I want to go home with you," said the king, "and see if it's true that everything's so much finer and more splendid. But if you're lying, then woe be unto you! I'm not saying any more, I'm not!"

"Well, you've really landed me in a fine mess!" said Per to the cat. "Now the king wants to come home with me; but my home — that's certainly no easy matter to find."

"Oh, don't worry about that," said the Cat. "You just follow where I lead."

Then they set out, first Per who drove behind the cat, who ran ahead, and the king with all his company.

Now when they had driven a good distance, they came to a big herd of pretty sheep, with wool so long that it almost reached the ground.

"If you'll say that this herd of sheep belongs to Squire Per, when the king asks you, you'll get this silver spoon," said the cat to the shepherd. She had taken the silver spoon from the king's manor.

Yes, he'd do it gladly.

So when the king came, he said to the shepherd, "Now I've never seen such a big herd of pretty sheep! Who owns it, my little lad?"

"Oh, it's Squire Per's, to be sure," said the boy.

In a little while they came to a big, big herd of fine brindled cows. They were so glossy they shone.

"If you'll say that this herd belongs to Squire Per, when the king asks you, you'll get this silver ladle," said the cat to the shepherdess. The cat had also taken the silver ladle from the king's manor.

"Yes, gladly," said the shepherdess.

So when the king came, he was quite astounded at the big, fine herd, for such a beautiful herd he had never seen before. He asked the shepherdess who owned those brindled cattle there.

"Oh, it's Squire Per," said the maiden.

They travelled a little farther, and then they came to a big, big herd of horses; they were the handsomest horses any one ever saw, big and fat, and six of each color — red, and white, and black.

"If you'll say that this herd of horses belongs to Squire Per, when the king asks you, you'll get this silver goblet," said the cat to the herder. She had also taken the goblet from the king's manor.

Yes, he'd do that all right, said the boy.

So when the king came, he was greatly astonished over that big, fine herd of horses; for he had never seen the like of such horses, he said. So he asked the herder whom these red, and white, and black horses belonged to.

"They're Squire Per's, to be sure," said the boy.

Now, when they had journeyed a good distance farther, they came to a castle. First there was a gate of brass, then one of silver, and then one of gold. The castle itself was of silver, and so splendid that it hurt the eyes, for the sun was shining full on it when they arrived. They went in, and the cat told Per to say he lived here. Inside, the castle was even more splendid

The king asked the shepherd boy whom the red and white and black horses belonged to.
"Why, they're Squire Per's," said the boy.

than outside: everything was of gold — chairs, tables and benches. And when
the king had gone about and looked at everything, both upstairs and down, he
was quite ashamed.

"Yes, Squire Per is better off than I, there's no use denying it," he said,
and then he wanted to take his leave. But Per bade him stay and eat supper
with him, and that the king did, but he was sour and grumpy the whole time.

While they were sitting at the table, the Troll, who owned the castle, came
and knocked on the gate.

"Who's in here eating my food and drinking my mead like swine?" shouted
the Troll.

As soon as the cat heard him, she ran out to the gate.

"Wait a bit, and I'll tell you what the farmer does with his winter rye,"
said the cat. "First the farmer ploughs his field, then he spreads out manure,
and then he ploughs it again!"

Just then the sun rose.

"Look around and you'll see a gloriously beautiful maiden behind you!"
said the cat to the Troll.

So the Troll turned, and when he caught sight of the sun he burst!

"Now everything here is yours," said the cat to Squire Per, "and you must
chop off my head at once! That's the only thing I demand for what I've done
for you."

"No!" said Squire Per, "I just won't do it!"

"Yes!" said the cat. "If you don't, I'll scratch out your eyes!"

Well, then Squire Per had to do it. Unwilling though he was, he chopped off the cat's head.

But at the same moment she turned into the loveliest Princess anyone could wish to set eyes on, and Squire Per fell head over heels in love with her.

"Yes, all this was mine before," said the princess, "but the Troll there bewitched me, so I had to be a cat at your parent's hut. Now you must do whatever you wish, whether you want me as your queen or not. For now you are king over the whole realm," said the princess.

Oh yes, it just could be that Squire Per wanted her as his queen. So there was a wedding and a feast which lasted eight days, and then I wasn't with Squire Per and his queen any longer, that's the truth.

"There's the key," he said.

THE KEY IN THE DISTAFF

There was once a rich farmer's lad, and he was going out wooing. He had heard tell of a maiden who was both comely and fair, excellent at keeping house, and a great hand at cooking. So he made his way there, for such a wife he wanted to have. It was plain enough to the folk at the farm on what errand he had come, so they invited him in to sit down on the bench, and chatted with him, as is the custom; and in addition they offered him a drink to stay his thirst while they got something ready to eat. They went in and out, so the suitor had time to have a look around in the parlor. Over in a corner he saw a spinning wheel, and the distaff was full of flax.

"Who is it who spins on that wheel?" asked the lad.

"Oh, that would be our daughter now, it would," said the old woman of the house.

"That's a mighty large bundle of flax," said the lad. "She certainly must take more than a day to spin that off," he said.

"Nothing of the kind!" said the old woman. "She does it easily in one, and maybe in less than that!"

Drawings by Erik Werenskiold

A maiden who was both comely and fair, excellent at keeping house, and a great hand at cooking.

That was more than he had bargained for, that anyone could spin in so short a time, thought the lad.

But when they were to carry in the food, they all went out together, and he was left in the parlor alone. Then he caught sight of a big, old key lying on the window sill. He took it and thrust it up inside the distaff, working it well into the flax. Then they ate and drank, and were on good terms; and when he felt he had been there long enough, he thanked them and went his way. They bade him come again soon, and that he promised, too. But he did not state his business, even though he thought pretty well of the girl.

After a while he came to the farm again; this time they received him even better than the first time. But when they had started talking, the old woman said, "Since the last time you were here something really strange happened! Our larder key has disappeared so completely that we haven't been able to find it again!"

The lad went over to the spinning wheel, which was standing there in the corner with the bundle of flax just as big as the last time, and reached up inside the distaff.

"There's the key," he said. "There's little to win on what you spin, when the spinning-day lasts from Michaelmas to Easter!"

Then he thanked them, and didn't state his business this time either.

THE BOY WITH THE BEER KEG

There was once a boy who had long served a man up north of the Dovre Mountains. This man was a master at brewing beer; it was so fantastically good that the like of it was nowhere to be found. When the time came for the boy to leave, and the man was to pay him the wages he had earned, he would have nothing but a keg of the Christmas beer.

Well, he got it and set out with it, and he carried it both far and long. But the longer he carried the keg, the heavier it grew; so he started looking about to see if anyone was coming that he could drink with, so that there could be less beer in it and the keg would grow lighter.

After a while he met an old man with a great beard.

"Good day," said the man.

"Good day yourself," said the boy.

"Where are *you* off to?" said the man.

"I'm looking for someone to drink with so I can make my keg lighter," said the boy.

"Can't you just as well drink with me as with another?" said the man. "I've travelled far and wide, so I'm both tired and thirsty."

"Why yes, so I can," said the boy, "but where do you come from, and what sort of a man are you?" he asked.

"I am Providence, and I come from above, I do," said the man.

"I won't drink with *you!*" said the boy. "For you make such a distinction between folk here in the world, and dole out justice so unequally, that some become rich and some unreasonably poor. No, I won't drink with *you!*" he said and trudged off again with his keg.

When he had gone a bit farther, the keg again became so heavy that he didn't think he could go on carrying it any longer unless someone came that he could drink with, so that there would be less beer in it.

Well, then he met an ugly, skinny man who came rushing along at a fast clip.

"Good day," said the man.

"Good day yourself," said the boy.

"Where are you off to?" said the man.

"Oh, I'm looking for someone to drink with so I can lighten my keg," said the boy.

Drawings by Erik Werenskiold

"Can't you just as well drink with me as with another?" said the man.

"Can't you just as well drink with me as with another?" said the man. "I've travelled both far and wide, and a drop of beer would do good in an old carcass," he said.

"Why yes, so I can," said the boy. "But what sort of a fellow are you, and where do you come from?" he asked.

"Me? I'm known well enough. I'm the Devil and I come from below, I do," said the man.

"Nay," said the boy, "you only plague and torment folk, and wherever there's any misery afoot, they always say it's your fault. Nay, I won't drink with *you!*" said the boy.

So he walked far, and farther than far again, until his beer keg had grown so heavy that he could not go on carrying it any longer. He started looking around again to see if anyone was coming that he could drink with, so the keg would grow lighter.

Well, after a long time, another man came along, and *he* was so dried up and skinny that it was an out-and-out miracle that he hung together.

"Good day," said the man.

"Good day yourself," said the boy.

"Where are you off to?" asked the man.

"I was going to see if I could find someone to drink with, so my keg will be a bit lighter. It's getting so heavy to carry," said the boy.

"Can't you just as well drink with me as with another?" said the man.

"Why yes, so I can," said the boy. "But what sort of a fellow are you?" he asked.

"They call me Death," said the man.

"I'll drink with *you*," said the boy, and put down the keg and started tapping beer into the mug. "You're a worthy man, for you make everyone alike, both rich and poor!"

So he drank with him, and Death thought it was a glorious drink; and, as the boy liked him well, they took turns drinking, so the beer went down and the keg grew lighter.

At last Death said, "I've never known a drink that tasted better or did me so much good as the beer you've just given me. I feel as if I'd been made like new and I don't know what I'm going to do to thank you for it."

But after pondering for a while, he said that the keg would never become empty, no matter how much they drank from it. And the beer that was in it

She was so dangerously ill that no doctor believed he could save her.

should turn into a magic medicine so that the boy could make the sick well again, better than any doctor. And then he said that, when he came in to one who was sick, Death would always be there, and appear to him; and, as a sure sign, when Death sat by the foot of the bed, he could save the sick with a health-giving drink from the keg. But when he sat by the head of the bed, then neither advice nor medicine would keep Death at bay.

The boy was soon renowned, and he was summoned from far and wide; and he helped multitudes back to health for whom there had been no hope. When he came in and saw where Death was sitting, he foretold either life or death, and he always prophesied correctly. He became both rich and powerful, and at last he was summoned to a king's daughter in a land far away. She was so danger-ously ill that no doctor believed he could save her, and so he was promised every-thing that he could wish and ask for, if only he could cure her. When he came into the room where the king's daughter lay, Death was sitting by the head of the bed, but he was dozing and nodding, and while he did she felt better.

"This is a question of life or death," said the doctor, "and indeed, there is no hope of recovery, if I see correctly," he said. But they said he must save her, even if it should cost both land and kingdom. So he looked at Death, and as he dozed off again, he signalled to the servants to turn the bed around in a hurry, so that Death was sitting by the foot, and as soon as this was done, he gave her the healing drink, so she was saved.

"Now you've cheated me!" said Death. "And now we're quits!"

"I had to if I was to win land and kingdom," said the boy.

"That won't help you much," said Death. "Your time is up, for now you belong to me."

"Well, if it has to be, then so let it be," said the boy. "But surely you'll let me say the Lord's Prayer first," he said.

Yes, that he could do, but he took good care not to say the Lord's Prayer. He said everything else, but "Our Father —" never came to his lips, and at last he thought he had cheated Death once and for all.

But when Death thought it had dragged out long enough, he went in one night and hung up a large board, with the Lord's Prayer on it, over the boy's bed. When the boy woke up, he started saying it, and didn't really come to his senses until he came to "Amen". But then it was too late.

"Now you've cheated me!" said Death.

THE COCK
AND THE FOX

Once upon a time there was a Cock who stood on a dunghill, crowing and flapping his wings. Then the Fox came along.

"Good day!" said the Fox. "I heard you crowing, all right. But can you stand on one leg and crow with your eyes closed as your father could?" he asked.

"That I can, both loud and long," said the Cock, and he stood on one leg. But he closed only one eye, and when he had done that, he preened himself and flapped his wings as though he had done something big.

"That was pretty," said the Fox. "It's almost as pretty as when the priest sings Mass in the church. But can you also stand on one leg and crow, and close both eyes at the same time? I hardly

Drawings by Erik Werenskiold

135

believe *you* can do that." said the Fox. "But your father, now — *he* was a fine fellow!"

"Oh, I can do that too!" said the Cock, and he stood on one leg and closed both eyes and crowed. Like a flash the Fox jumped on him, seized him by the neck, and slung him on his back, so he didn't finish crowing before he was being whisked off to the woods as fast as the Fox could run.

When they came to the shade of a shaggy old fir tree, the Fox hurled the Cock to the ground, put his foot on his breast, and was just going to take a good bite.

"You're not as devout as your father was," said the Cock. "He crossed himself and blessed his food, he did."

Well, the Fox wanted to be devout too. So he let go his hold, and was going to fold his paws and pray. And pop! the Cock flew up into a tree!

"You certainly won't get away with that!" said the Fox to himself. Then he went away and came back with a couple of chips left by the woodcutters. The Cock peered and peered to see what *that* could be.

"What have you got there?" he said.

"They're letters I've received from the Pope in Rome," said the Fox. "Won't you help me read them, for I don't know how to myself."

"I'd be more than glad to, but I dare not now," said the Cock. "For there comes a hunter; I can see him behind a tree. I see 'im! I see 'im!" he cried.

When the Fox heard what the Cock was cackling about the hunter, he took to his heels and ran off as fast as he could go.

This time it was the Cock who turned the tables on the Fox.

NOT DRIVING AND NOT RIDING

There was once a king's son who had wooed a maiden. But when they had come to an understanding and were on good terms, he lost all interest in the girl. Now he didn't want to marry her because she wasn't good enough for him. And so he thought he would try to be quit of her. But he said he would take her all the same, if she could come to him

> not driving
> and not riding,
> not walking
> and not sliding,
> not hungry
> and not full,

Drawing by Th. Kittelsen

> not naked
> and not clad,
> not by day,
> and not by night.

For he believed she could never manage that.

She took three barleycorns and bit them in two, so she was not full, but she was not fasting either. And then she draped a net over herself, so she was

> not naked
> and not clad.

She then took a ram and seated herself on its back, so her feet dragged along the ground. Thus she shuffled forward, and then she was

> not driving
> and not riding,
> not walking
> and not sliding.

And it was in the twilight between night and day.

When she reached the guards, she asked to be allowed to talk with the prince, but they would not let her in because she looked such a sight. But the prince was awakened by all the commotion, and came to the window. She shuffled across and wrung off one of the ram's horns; and she took it and, standing up on the ram's back, she knocked on the window with it. So they had to open up and make her into a princess.

THE GOLDEN CASTLE
THAT HUNG IN THE AIR

There was once a man who had three sons. When he died, the two eldest decided to go out into the world to try their luck; but they wouldn't take the youngest with them at any price.

"You, now," they said, "you're no good for anything but sitting and holding the pine torches, poking in the ashes and blowing on the coals!"

"Well, well, I'll just have to go by myself, I will," said the Ash Lad. "Then I won't be at odds with my company, either!"

The two set out, and after travelling for some days, they came to a great forest. There they sat down to rest and eat some of the food they had brought with them, for they were both tired and hungry. As they sat there, an old hag came up through a tuft of grass and begged for a little food. She was so old and feeble that her mouth twitched and her head quivered, and she had to support herself on a staff. She hadn't had a crumb of bread in her mouth in a hundred years, she said; but the boys only laughed and went on eating, and said that as long as she'd kept body and soul together for so long, as like as not she'd be able to hold out without eating up their crumbs. Besides, they had little to share and nothing to spare.

When they had eaten their fill and rested, they set out again, and at last they came to the king's manor; there they were given jobs as serving-men — both of them.

A short while after they had left home, the Ash Lad gathered together the crumbs his brothers had cast aside, and put them in his little knapsack; and he took the old musket which had no bolt, for he thought it would come in handy on the way. Then he set out. When he had walked for some days, he too came to the thick forest through which his brothers had travelled, and when he was tired and hungry, he sat down under a tree to rest and have a little to eat. But he had his eyes open, and as he took up his knapsack he caught sight of a picture hanging on a tree, and on it was painted a young maiden, or princess, who was so lovely that he could not take his eyes off her. He forgot both

Drawings by Th. Kittelsen

139

food and knapsack, and took down the picture, and sat staring intently at it. All of a sudden the old hag came up through the tuft of grass, her mouth twitching and her head quivering, and supporting herself on a staff, and she begged him for a little food, for she hadn't had a crumb of bread in her mouth in a hundred years, she said.

"Then it's time you had a little, Old Mother," said the boy, and he gave her some bread crumbs. The old hag said that no one had called her 'Mother' in a hundred years, and she was certainly going to do him a favor in return. She gave him a ball of grey wool, which he only had to roll along in front of him and he would come to any place he wanted to. But he mustn't bother with the picture, she said, it would only get him into trouble. The Ash Lad thought this was all very well, but he couldn't leave the painting behind, so he took it under his arm, and rolled the ball of yarn ahead of him, and it wasn't long before he came to the king's manor where his brothers were serving. There he too begged for a serving-job. They replied that they had no work for him, as they had recently taken on two serving-boys, but he begged so hard that at last he was allowed to help the stablemaster, and be trained to groom the horses. This the Ash Lad was most willing to do, for he was fond of horses; and as he was both quick and clever, he soon learned to tend and take care of them, and it wasn't long before everyone in the king's manor grew fond of him. But every spare moment he would be up looking at the picture, for he had hung it in a corner of the hayloft.

His brothers were idle and lazy, so they were often soundly beaten, and when they saw that the Ash Lad was getting along better than they were, they grew jealous of him, and told the stablemaster that he was an idol worshipper — he prayed to a picture and not to Our Lord. Even though the stablemaster thought well of the boy, it wasn't long before he told the king. But the king only snapped at him; these days he was always downcast and sorrowful, for his daughters had been carried off by a Troll. But they dinned it into the king's ears for so long that at last he wanted to find out what the boy was up to. When he came to the hayloft and set eyes on the picture, he saw it was a painting of his youngest daughter. When the Ash Lad's brothers heard that, they were ready with a story at once, and said to the stablemaster, "If only our brother were willing, he's said he could get the king back his daughter!" You may be sure that it wasn't long before the stablemaster went to the king and told him *that*, and when the king heard it, he shouted for the Ash Lad and said, "Your brothers say you can get my daughter back, and now you shall do so!"

The Ash Lad replied that he never knew it was the king's daughter before the king had said so himself, and if he could free her and bring her back, he would certainly do his best; but he must have two days to consider it and fit himself out. This he was given.

The boy took out the ball of grey wool and threw it down on the road, and it rolled ahead, and he went after it until he came to the old hag who had given it to him. He asked her what he should do, and she said he was to take his old

140

The boy took out the ball of grey wool and threw it down on the road.

musket, and three hundred crates full of spikes and horseshoe nails, and three hundred barrels of barley, and three hundred barrels of groats, and three hundred butchered pigs, and three hundred ox carcasses, and roll the ball along the road until he met a raven and a Troll-child, and then he would get there all right, for those two were of her kin. Well, the boy did as she said: he looked in at the king's manor, and took his old musket, and asked the king for spikes, and beef, and pork, and horses and men and carts to transport them. The king thought it was asking a lot, but as long as he could get his daughter back, he would give him whatever he needed, even if it were half the kingdom, he said.

When the boy had fitted himself out, he rolled the ball along the road again, and he hadn't gone many days before he came to a high mountain. There in a fir tree sat a raven. The Ash Lad walked until he stood directly beneath it, and pretended to take aim with his musket.

"Nay, don't shoot! Don't shoot me and I'll help you!" shrieked the raven.

"I've never heard anyone brag about roast raven," said the boy, "and since you're so anxious about your life, I may as well spare you." So he threw the musket aside, and the raven came flying down and said, "Up on this mountain is a Troll-child who has got lost and can't find his way down again. I'll help you up so you can take the youngster home, and get yourself a reward which should come in very handy. When you get there, the Troll will offer you all the finest things he has, but you must pay no attention to that. You must take nothing but the little grey donkey which is standing behind the stable door."

Then the raven took the boy on his back, and flew up onto the mountain with him, and put him down there. After a while, he heard the Troll-child whimpering and carrying on because he couldn't find his way down again. The boy talked kindly to him, and they became friends and were soon on the best of terms, and he promised to help the Troll-child down. He was going to take

141

him home to the Troll Manor, so that he wouldn't get lost on the way. Then they went to the raven, and he took them both on his back and carried them straight to the Mountain Troll.

When the Troll laid eyes on his child again, he was so glad that he quite forgot himself, and told the boy to come in with him and take whatever he wanted, because he had saved his son. He offered him both gold and silver, and all sorts of rare and costly things, but the boy said he would rather have a horse. Yes, he should have a horse, said the Troll, and so out to the stable they went. It was full of the finest horses. They shone like the sun and the moon, but the boy felt they were all too big for him. So he peeped behind the stable door, and caught sight of the little grey donkey standing there. "That's the one I want!" he said. "That's more my size. If I fall off, I'm not far from the ground." The Troll was loath to lose the donkey, but as long as he'd given his promise, he had to stand by it. So the boy got the donkey, with saddle and bridle and all, and then he hurried on his way.

They journeyed through forest and field, over mountain and broad moors. When they had travelled farther than far, the donkey asked if the boy could see anything.

"No, I see nothing but a high mountain which looks purple in the distance."

"Well, we're going through that mountain," said the donkey.

"Am I to believe that?" said the boy.

When they came to the mountain, a unicorn came charging towards them as though it wanted to eat them alive.

"Now I think I'm almost afraid," said the boy.

"Oh, not at all," said the donkey. "Unload a couple of score of ox carcasses, and ask it to bore a hole and break a road through the mountain."

The boy did so. When the unicorn had eaten its fill, they promised it a couple of score of butchered pigs if it would go ahead and bore a hole through the mountain so that they could get through. When the unicorn heard that, it bored a hole and broke through the mountain, so fast that it was all they could do to keep up with it. And when it had finished, they threw it a couple of score of pig carcasses.

When they had come safely through this, they journeyed a long way through many a land, and then they journeyed through forest and field, over mountain and wild moors again.

"Do you see anything now?" asked the donkey.

"Now I see nothing but sky and wild mountains," said the boy. So they journeyed far, and farther than far, and when they came higher up, the mountains became more level and flatter, so they could see farther around them on every side.

"Do you see anything now?" asked the donkey.

"Yes, I see something a long, long way off," said the boy. "It's sparkling and twinkling like a tiny star."

"It's certainly not so little, though," said the donkey. When they had journeyed far, and farther than far again, it asked, "Do you see anything now?"

142

"Yes, I see something a long, long way off," said the boy. "It's sparkling and twinkling like a tiny star."

"Yes, now I see something a long way off. It's shining like a moon," said the boy.

"That's no moon," said the donkey. "That's the silver castle we're going to," it said. "Now, when we get there, we shall find three dragons lying on guard by the gate. They haven't been awake for a hundred years, so the moss has grown over their eyes."

"I think I'll almost be afraid of them, I will," said the boy.

"Oh, not at all!" said the donkey. "You must wake up the youngest and toss down its gullet a couple of score of ox carcasses and butchered pigs. Then I dare say it'll talk to the other two, and you'll be allowed to enter the castle."

They journeyed far, and farther than far, before they arrived at the castle, but when they got there, it was both large and splendid, and everything they saw was made of silver. And outside the gate lay the dragons blocking the way so that no one could get in. But it had been quiet and peaceful, and they hadn't been disturbed with much during their watch, for they were so overgrown with moss that no one could see what they were made of, and alongside them a small forest had started growing between the mounds of moss. The boy woke the smallest of them, and it started rubbing its eyes and picking off the moss. When at last the dragon saw that there were folk there, it came towards him with its jaws open wide, but the boy was ready, and tossed ox carcasses and threw pigs down its gullet, until it had eaten its fill and had become a little more reasonable to talk to. The boy asked it to wake up the others, and tell them to move aside so that he could enter the castle. But the dragon said it dared not and would not do so, to begin with; they hadn't been awake or tasted food for a hundred years. It was afraid they would thrash about in a daze, and devour both living and dead in their confusion. The boy said it needn't worry, for they could leave behind a hundred ox carcasses and a hundred pigs, and go away for a bit. Then they could eat their fill, and collect their wits by the time they came back again. Well, the dragon agreed to this, and so they did just that. But before the dragons were properly awake and had got the moss off their eyes, they flew around and thrashed about, and snapped at all and sundry, and it was all the youngest dragon could do to keep out of harm's way until they had got wind of the meat. Then they gobbled oxen and pig carcasses whole, and ate their fill. After that they were pretty tame and good-natured, and let the boy walk past them into the castle. Inside everything was so splendid that he could hardly believe anything could be so fine anywhere. But it was empty of people, for he went from room to room, and opened all the doors, but he saw no one. Well, at last he peeped in through the door of a chamber he had not seen before, and inside sat a princess spinning, and she was so pleased and happy when she caught sight of him.

"Nay, nay! Dare Christian folk come here?" she shouted. "But you'd certainly better go again, or else the Troll may kill you. For a Troll with three heads lives here!"

The boy said he wasn't going to move even if the Troll had seven. When the princess heard that, she wanted him to try to swing the big, rusty sword

144

which hung behind the door. But he couldn't swing it; he couldn't even lift it.

"Well," said the princess, "if you can't manage it, you'll have to take a swig from that flask hanging beside it, for that's what the Troll does when he's going out to use it!"

The boy took a couple of swigs, and now he could swing the sword as though it were a pancake turner.

All at once the Troll came rushing up. "Huh! I smell the smell of Christian flesh!" he shrieked.

"So you do!" said the boy, "But you needn't snort so loud. You won't be bothered by that smell any more," he said, and then he chopped off all his heads.

The princess was as happy as though she had been given something fine. But after a while she began to pine; she longed for her sister, who had been carried off by a Troll with six heads, and now lived in a castle of gold which was three hun-

The golden castle that hung in the air.

dred miles beyond the world's end. The boy wasn't put out one bit. He could fetch both princess and castle, and so he took the sword and the flask, mounted the donkey, and bade the dragons follow him, and carry the meat, and the pork and the spikes.

When they had journeyed a while, and travelled a long, long way over land and sea, the donkey said one day, "Do you see anything?"

"I see nothing but land, and water and sky, and high crags," said the boy. So they travelled far, and farther than far.

"Do you see anything now?" said the donkey.

Yes, when he looked carefully ahead, he saw something far, far away; it shone like a tiny star, said the boy.

145

"I dare say it'll get bigger," said the donkey. When they had journeyed a long way again, it asked, "Do you see anything now?"

"Now I see it shining like a moon," said the boy.

"Well, well," said the donkey. When they had gone far, and farther than far, over land and sea, over hill and moor again, the donkey asked, "Do you see anything now?"

"Now I think it's shining almost like the sun," said the boy.

"Well, that's the golden castle we're going to," said the donkey, "but outside lies a serpent which bars the way and keeps watch."

"I think I'll be afraid of it," said the boy.

"Oh, not at all," said the donkey. "We'll have to pile layers of twigs over it, and in between, rows of horseshoe nails, and set it on fire. Then we'll probably be rid of it."

At last they came to where the castle hung, but the serpent lay stretched out in front of it and barred the way. Then the boy gave the dragons a good meal of ox and pig carcasses so they would help him; and then they spread over the serpent a layer of twigs and wood, and a layer of spikes and horseshoe nails, until they had used up the three hundred crates which they had. And when that was done, they set fire to it and burned the serpent alive.

When that was done, one of the dragons flew underneath and lifted the castle up, while the two others flew high up in the sky and loosened the chains from the hooks they were hanging on, and set it down on the ground. The boy went inside, and found everything was even more splendid than in the silver castle, but he saw no one until he came into the innermost room. There on a golden bed lay the princess. She was sleeping as soundly as if she were dead; but she wasn't dead, even though he wasn't man enough to wake her, for she was as red and white as milk and blood. Just as the boy stood there looking at her, the Troll came rushing in. Hardly had he put his first head through the door before he started shrieking, "Huff! I smell the smell of Christian flesh!"

"Perhaps," said the boy, "but you needn't snort so loud about it. You won't be bothered by that smell for long!" he said, and then he chopped off all his heads as though they were set on cabbage stalks. Then the dragons put the golden castle on their backs, and flew home with it — they weren't long on the way, I can tell you — and set it down beside the silver castle so that it shone both far and wide.

When the princess from the silver castle came to the window in the morning and caught sight of it, she was so happy that she ran over to the golden castle that very minute. But when she saw her sister lying asleep as though she were dead, she told the boy that they couldn't bring her to life before they had fetched the Waters of Life and Death, which were kept in two wells on either side of a golden castle which hung in the air, nine hundred miles beyond the world's end. And there lived the third sister. Well, there was no other way out, thought the boy, he would have to fetch that, too, and it wasn't long before he was on the

146

way. And he travelled far, and farther than far, through many kingdoms, through field and forest, over mountain and moor, over land and sea. At last he came to the world's end, and still he travelled far and long, over heath and hill and high crags.

"Do you see anything?" asked the donkey one day.

"I see nothing but heaven and earth," said the boy.

"Do you see anything now?" asked the donkey after some days.

"Yes, now I think I can make out something high up and far away, just like a tiny star."

"It's certainly not so tiny, though," said the donkey. When they had gone a while again, it asked, "Do you see anything now?"

"Yes, now I think it's shining like a moon."

"Oh indeed?" said the donkey.

So they travelled a few days more. "Do you see anything now?" said the donkey.

"Yes, now it's shining like the sun," replied the boy.

"That's where we're going," said the donkey. "That's the golden castle which hangs in the air. A princess lives there who has been carried off by a Troll with nine heads. But all the wild animals in the world lie on guard, and bar the way to it," said the donkey.

"Huff! I almost think I'll be afraid now," said the boy.

"Oh, not at all!" said the donkey. And it said that there was no danger as long as he didn't stay there, but left as soon as he had filled his pitchers with the water. For the castle could only be entered for one hour during the day, and that was at high noon. And if he couldn't finish in that time, and come away, the wild animals would tear him into a thousand pieces.

Yes, he would do that, said the boy; he certainly wouldn't wait too long.

At twelve o'clock they arrived. All the wild and wicked beasts were lying like a fence outside the gate and on both sides of the road. But they slept like logs, and there wasn't one which so much as lifted a paw. The boy went between them, and took good care not to tread on toe nor tip of tail, and filled his pitchers with the Waters of Life and Death, and while he did so, he looked at the castle which was made of purest gold. It was the finest he had ever seen, and he thought it must be even finer inside. "Pooh! I have plenty of time," thought the Ash Lad. "I can always look around for half an hour," and so he opened the door and went in. Inside it was finer than fine. He went from one magnificent room to another, and it was closely hung with gold and pearls, and all the costliest things there were. But no people were to be found. At last he came into a chamber, where a princess lay asleep on a golden bed as though she were dead. But she was as fine as the finest queen, and as red and white as blood and snow, and so beautiful that he had never seen anything as beautiful, save her picture! For she it was who was painted there. The boy forgot both the water he was to fetch, and the animals, and the whole castle, and only looked at the princess. And he thought he could never gaze his fill at her, but she slept like one dead, and he couldn't wake her.

147

Towards evening the Troll came rushing in, and crashed and banged all the gates and doors so that the whole castle rang. "Huff! Here I smell the smell of Christian flesh!" he said, and stuck his first head through the door.

"I dare say you do," said the boy, "but you needn't snort till the bellows split for that. You won't be bothered by that smell for long," he said, and with that he chopped off all its heads. But when he was finished, he was so tired that he couldn't keep his eyes open. So he lay down in the bed beside the princess, and she slept both night and day as though she would never wake. But around midnight she woke for a moment, and then she told him that he had freed her, but she must remain there for three more years. If she didn't return to him then, he would have to come and fetch her.

He didn't wake up until the clock had started on another day, and he heard the donkey braying and carrying on so that he thought it best to set out for home. Before leaving he clipped a piece out of the princess' gown to take with him. But what with one thing or another, he had hung about there so long that the animals were stirring and beginning to wake up. By the time he had mounted the donkey, they were closing in around him until he thought things looked really dangerous. But the donkey told him to sprinkle some drops of the Water of Death on them. This he did, and they all fell down on the spot and moved not a limb again.

On the way home the donkey said to the boy, "Mark my words, when you come into honor and glory, you'll forget me and what I've done for you, so I'll be down on my knees with hunger." No, that would never happen, thought the boy.

When he came back to the princess with the Water of Life, she sprinkled a few drops on her sister so that she woke up, and then there was joy and rapture, as you might know.

Then they went home to the king, and he too was happy and glad to have them with him again. But he pined and pined for the three years to be up, when his youngest daughter was to come home. He made the boy, who had fetched the two princesses, a mighty man, so that he was the first in the land next to the king. But there were many who were jealous because he had become such an important fellow, and there was one — he was called the Red Knight — who, they said, wanted to have the eldest princess. He got her to sprinkle a little of the Water of Death on the boy so that he fell asleep.

When the three years were up, and the fourth year was well begun, a foreign warship came sailing, and on it was the third sister, and she had with her a three-year-old child. She sent word to the king's manor that she wouldn't set foot on shore before they sent down the man who had come to the golden castle and freed her. So they sent down one of the highest persons at the king's court, and when he stepped on board the ship, he swept off his hat to the princess, and bowed and scraped.

"Can that be your father, my son?" said the princess to the child, who was playing with a golden apple.

"No, my father doesn't crawl like a cheese maggot!" said the boy.

148

Then they sent another of the same sort, and that was the Red Knight. But he fared no better than the first, and the princess sent word by him that if they didn't send the right one, it would go badly with them all. When they heard that, they had to wake up the boy with the Water of Life, and then he went down to the ship to see the princess. But *he* didn't bow too much, I can tell you. He only nodded and pulled out the piece he had clipped from her gown in the golden castle.

"That's my father!" shouted the child, and gave him the golden apple he was playing with. Then there was great rejoicing over the whole kingdom, and the old king was the happiest of them all for his favorite child had returned. But when it came to light what the Red Knight and the eldest princess had done to the boy, the king wanted them each rolled in a spiked barrel. But the Ash Lad and the youngest princess pleaded for them, and so they were spared.

One day, as they were getting ready to celebrate the wedding, the Ash Lad stood looking out of the window. It was getting on towards spring and they were letting out the horses and the cattle, and the last animal to leave the stable was the donkey. But it was so starved that it crawled through the stable door on its knees. Then he felt so ashamed at having forgotten it that he went down and didn't know what he could do to help. But the donkey said the best thing he could do was to chop off its head. This he was most unwilling to do, but the donkey begged so hard that at last he had to. And at the same moment as the head fell, the Troll-spell which had been cast over it was broken, and there stood the handsomest prince that anyone could wish to see. He got the second princess, and they celebrated a wedding that was the talk of seven kingdoms.

Then a house they did build,
And shoes they did patch,
And wee princes they had
From cellar to thatch.

WHITE-BEAR-KING-VALEMON

There was once, as well could be, a king. He had two daughters who were mean and ugly, but the third was as fair and sweet as the bright day, and the king and all were fond of her. She once dreamed about a golden wreath, which was so lovely that she couldn't live unless she got it. But as she couldn't get it, she began to pine and could not speak for sorrow. And when the king found out it was the wreath she was grieving for, he had one made almost like the one the princess had dreamed of, and sent it out to goldsmiths in every land and asked them to make one like it. They worked both day and night, but some of the wreaths she threw away, and others she wouldn't even look at. Then one day, when she was in the forest, she caught sight of a white bear, which had the wreath she had dreamed of between its paws and was playing with it. And she wanted to buy it.

No! It wasn't to be had for money, but only in return for herself. Well, life wasn't worth living without it, she said; it didn't matter where she went or who she got, if only she got the wreath. And so they agreed that he was to fetch her in three days' time, and that would be a Thursday.

Drawings by Th. Kittelsen

When she came home with the wreath, everyone was glad because she was happy again, and the king felt sure that it would be a simple matter to keep a white bear at bay. On the third day, the whole army was posted round the castle to deal with him. But when the white bear came, there was no one who could hold his ground against him, for no weapon could make any effect on him. He knocked them down right and left until they were lying in heaps. This, thought the king, was proving downright disastrous; so he sent out his eldest daughter, and the white bear took her on his back and rushed off with her.

When they had travelled far, and farther than far, the white bear asked, "Have you ever sat softer, have you ever seen clearer?"

"Yes, on my mother's lap I sat softer, in my father's court I saw clearer," she said.

"Well, you're not the right one then," said the white bear, and chased her home again.

The next Thursday he came again, and did just as he had done before. The army was out with orders to deal with the white bear. But neither iron nor steel bit on him, so he mowed them down like grass until the king had to ask him to stop. And then he sent out his next eldest daughter, and the white bear took her up on his back and rushed off with her.

When they had travelled far, and farther than far, the white bear asked, "Have you ever sat softer, have you ever seen clearer?"

"Yes," she said, "in my father's court I saw clearer, on my mother's lap I sat softer."

"Well, you're not the right one then," said the white bear, and chased her home again.

On the third Thursday he came again. This time he fought even harder than before, until the king thought he couldn't let him knock down the whole army, and so he gave him his third daughter. Then he took her on his back and travelled away, far, and farther than far, and when they had reached the forest, he asked her, as he had asked the others, if she had ever sat softer and seen clearer.

"*No, never!*" she said.

"Well, *you're* the right one," he said.

So they came to a castle which was so fine that the castle her father lived in was like the meanest cottage in comparison. There she was to stay, and live well, and she was to have nothing else to do but see to it that the fire never went out. The bear was away during the day, but at night he was with her, and then he was a man. For three years all went as well as could be. But each year she had a child, which he took and rushed away with as soon as it had come into the world. So she became more and more downcast, and asked if she couldn't be allowed to go home and see her parents. Yes, there was no objection to that; but first she must promise that she would listen to what her father *said*, but not to what her mother wanted her to *do*. So she went home, and when they were alone with her, and she had told them how she was getting on, her mother

"Have you ever sat softer, have you ever seen clearer?"
"*No, never!*" she said.

wanted to give her a candle to take with her so she could see what the bear was like when he turned into a man at night. But her father said no, she shouldn't do that. "It will only do more harm than good."

But no matter how it was or was not, she took the candle stub with her when she left. The first thing she did, when he had fallen asleep, was to light it and shine it on him. He was so handsome that she thought she

So the king's daughter set off through the forest, and the next morning she came to another cottage.

could never gaze her fill at him; but, as she shone the light, a drop of hot tallow dripped onto his forehead, and so he awoke.

"What have you done?" he said. "Now you have brought misfortune on us both. There was no more than a month left; if you had only held out I would have been freed, for a Troll-hag has bewitched me, so that I'm a white bear during the day. But now it's over with us. Now I have to go there and take her."

She cried and carried on, but he had to go and go he would. So she asked if she could go with him. That was out of the question, he said, but when he rushed off in his bearskin, she seized hold of the fur all the same, flung herself up on his back, and held on fast. Then they were off over mountain and hill, through grove and thicket, until her clothes were torn off, and she was so dead tired that she let go her hold, and knew no more. When she awoke, she was in a great forest, and so she set out on her way again, but she didn't know where her path led. At last she came to a cottage where there were two womenfolk, an old crone and a pretty little girl.

The king's daughter asked if they had seen anything of White-Bear-King-Valemon.

"Yes, he rushed by here early today, but he was going so fast that you won't catch up with him again," they said.

The little girl scampered about, and clipped and played with a pair of golden scissors, which were such that pieces of silk and strips of velvet flew about her

153

if she but clipped in the air. Wherever the scissors were, clothes were never lacking.

"But this poor woman, who has to journey so far and on such rough roads, she'll have to toil hard," said the little girl. "She has more need of these scissors than I, to cut clothes for herself," she said, and then she asked if she could give her the scissors. Yes, that she could.

So the king's daughter set off through the forest which never came to an end, all that day and night. And the next morning she came to another cottage. Here there were also two womenfolk, an old crone and a little girl.

"Good day," said the king's daughter. "Have you seen anything of White-Bear-King-Valemon?" she asked.

"Were you to have had him, maybe?" said the old woman.

That it was.

"Why, yes, he rushed by here yesterday, but he went so fast that you won't catch up with him," she said.

The little girl was playing about on the floor with a flask, which was such that it poured out whatever they wanted, and wherever the flask was, drink was never lacking.

"But this poor woman, who has to journey so far and on such rough roads, she'll be thirsty and suffer many other hardships," said the little girl, and then she asked if she could give her the flask. Why, yes, that she could.

So the king's daughter got the flask, said her thanks, and set out again, walking through the same forest, all that day and night. On the third morning she came to a cottage, and there were an old woman and a little girl.

"Good day," said the king's daughter.

"Good day to you," said the old woman.

"Have you seen anything of White-Bear-King-Valemon?" she said.

"Maybe you were to have had him?" said the old woman. Yes, that it was.

"Why, yes, he rushed past here yesterday evening; but he went so fast that you'll never catch up with him again," she said.

The little girl was playing on the floor with a cloth that was such that, whenever they said to it, "Cloth, spread thyself, and deck thyself with every good dish!" it did so. And wherever the cloth was, good food was never lacking.

"But this poor old woman, who has to journey so far and on such rough roads," said the little girl, "she may well both starve and suffer many other hardships, so she'll have more need of this cloth than I," she said, and then she asked if she could give her the cloth. That she could.

So the king's daughter took the cloth and said her thanks, and set off. Far, and farther than far, through the forest all that day and night she went. In the morning she came to a mountain spur which was as steep as a wall, and so high and so wide that no end could she see. There was a cottage there too, and, when she came in, the first thing she said was,

"Good day, have you seen whether White-Bear-King-Valemon has travelled this way?"

"Good day to you," said the old woman. "Maybe it was you who was to have had him?" she asked That it was.

"Yes, he rushed up the mountain here three days ago; but nestlings can't get up there," she said.

This cottage was full of little children, and they

He was in no condition to wake up for all the king's daughter shouted and cried.

all clung to their mother's apron-strings and cried for food. The old woman put a kettle full of pebbles on the fire. The king's daughter asked what was the good of that. They were so poor, said the old woman, that they could afford neither food nor clothes, and it was so hard to hear the children crying for a bite to eat. But when she put the kettle on the fire, and said, "Now the apples will soon be done," it seemed to deaden their hunger, and they were patient for a while. It wasn't long before the king's daughter got out the cloth and the flask, as you can imagine, and when the children were fed and happy, she clipped out clothing for them with the golden scissors.

"Well," said the old woman of the house, "since you've been so heartily kind to me and my children, it would be a shame not to do what we can to try to help you up the mountain. My husband is really a master smith. Now you just rest until he comes back, and I'll get him to forge claws for your hands and feet, and then you can try to crawl up."

When the smith came, he started on the claws right away, and the next morning they were ready. She had no time to wait, but said her thanks, fastened the claws on her hands and crept and crawled up the mountainside the whole day and night, and, just when she was so tired that she didn't think she could lift her hand again, but felt she would sink to the ground, she got to the top. There was a plain, with fields and meadows so big and wide that she had never imagined anything so broad and so smooth, and close by there was a castle filled with workers of every kind, who toiled like ants in an anthill.

"What is going on here?" asked the king's daughter.

Well, this was where she lived, the Troll-hag who had bewitched White-Bear-King-Valemon, and in three days she was to wed him. The King's daughter asked if she could talk with her. No, not likely! That was out-and-out impossible. So she sat down outside the window, and started clipping with the golden scissors, and velvet and silken clothing flew about like a snowflurry. When the Troll-hag caught sight of that, she wanted to buy the scissors. "For no matter how the tailors toil, it's no use," she said, "there are too many to be clothed."

The scissors weren't for sale, said the king's daughter. But the Troll-hag could have them, if she would let her sleep with her sweetheart tonight. She could certainly do that, said the Troll-hag, but *she* would lull him to sleep herself, and wake him up herself. When he had gone to bed, she gave him a sleeping potion, so he was in no condition to wake up, for all the king's daughter shouted and cried.

The next day the king's daughter went outside the windows again, sat down and started pouring from the flask; it flowed like a brook, both beer and wine, and it never ran dry. When the Troll-hag laid eyes on that, she wanted to buy it; for "no matter how much they toil at the brewing and distilling, it's no use. There are too many to drink," she said. It wasn't for sale for money, said the king's daughter, but if she would let her sleep with her sweetheart tonight, she would give it to her. Yes, that she could certainly do, said the Troll-hag, but *she* would lull him to sleep herself, and wake him up herself. When he had gone to bed, she gave him a sleeping potion again, so the King's daughter had no better luck that night either. He couldn't be awakened, for all she cried and shouted. But that night one of the artisans was working in the room next door. He heard her crying in there, and he guessed what had really happened, and the next day he told the prince that *she* must have come, the king's daughter who was to have freed him.

The next day went just like the others — with the cloth as with the scissors and the flask. When it was dinner time, the king's daughter went outside the castle, pulled out the cloth, and said, "Cloth, spread thyself and deck thyself with every good dish!" Then there was enough food for a hundred men, but the king's daughter sat down alone. When the Troll-hag caught sight of the cloth, she wanted to buy it, for "no matter how much they cook and bake, it's no use. There are too many mouths to feed," she said. It wasn't for sale for money, said the king's daughter, but if she would let her sleep with her sweetheart tonight, she could have it. She could certainly do that, said the Troll-hag, but *she* would lull him to sleep herself, and wake him up herself. When he had gone to bed, she came with a sleeping potion, but this time he was on his guard, and fooled her. The Troll-hag didn't trust him any more than just so far, she didn't, for she took a darning needle and stuck it right through his arm, to see if he were sleeping soundly enough. But no matter how much it hurt, he didn't move, and then the king's daughter was allowed to come in to him.

Now this was all very well, but they must get rid of the Troll-hag before he would be free. So he got the carpenters to make a trap-door on the bridge which the bridal procession was to cross, for it was the custom there that the bride should ride first in the procession. When the Troll-hag started across the bridge with all her Troll-hag bridesmaids, the planks under them dropped open and they fell through. Then King Valemon and the king's daughter and all the wedding guests rushed back to the castle, and took as much of the Troll-hag's gold and money as they could carry, and then rushed off to his country to hold the real wedding. But on the way, King Valemon stopped in and fetched the three little girls, and now she found out why he had taken the children from her — it was so that they could help her find him. So they caroused at the wedding both lustily and long.

"GOOD DAY, FELLOW!" "AXE HANDLE!"

There was once a ferryman who was so deaf that he could neither hear nor make out what anyone said to him. He had an old wife, and two sons and a daughter, and they didn't trouble themselves about the man, but lived merrily and well, as long as there was anything to live on, and afterwards they bought on credit from the innkeeper, and gave parties and feasts every day.

When no one would give them any more credit, the bailiff was coming to seize their goods to pay for what they had borrowed and wasted. So the old woman and the children went to her kin, and left the deaf man behind alone to receive the bailiff and his man.

The man poked and pottered about the place, and wondered what the bailiff wanted to ask about, and what he should say when he came.

"I can start whittling away at something," he said to himself. "Then he'll ask me about it. I'll start on an axe handle. Then he'll ask me what *that's* going to be, and I'll say:

'Axe handle!'

Then he'll ask me how long it's going to be, so I'll say:

'Up to this knot!'

Then he'll ask where the ferry is, and I'll say:

'I'm going to tar her. She's lying down on the shore, cracked at both ends!'

Then he'll ask: 'Where's that old grey mare of yours?' So I'll say:

'She's out in the stall, big with foal!'

Then he'll ask: 'Where's your cattle and your cowshed?' And I'll say:

'That's not far away. When you get up the hill, you're there in no time!'"

This, he thought, was well and carefully thought out.

After a while the bailiff came. He was certain enough of the way, but his man had taken another road by way of the inn, and was still sitting there drinking.

"Good day, fellow!" said the bailiff.

"Axe handle!" said the ferryman.

Drawing by Th. Kittelsen

"Good day, fellow!" "Axe handle!"

"Ah so —," said the bailiff. "How far is it to the inn?" he asked.

"Up to this knot!" said the man and pointed a bit up the axe handle.

The bailiff shook his head and stared hard at him.

"Where's your old woman, fellow?" he said.

"I'm going to tar her," said the ferryman. "She's lying down on the shore, cracked at both ends!"

"Where's your daughter?"

"Oh, she's out in the stall, big with foal!" He thought he was answering both wisely and well for himself.

"Oh, go to the devil, fool that you are!" said the bailiff.

"Well, that's not far. Once you get up the hill, you're there in no time!" said the man.

THE TABBY WHO WAS SUCH A GLUTTON

There was once a man who had a Tabby, and she was so terribly large and such a glutton that he couldn't keep her any longer. So she was to go to the river with a stone around her neck, but first she was given a good meal. The old woman set a bowl of porridge and a little trough of drippings in front of her. The Tabby gobbled it down, and then jumped out through the window. The man was in the barn threshing.

"Good day to you, man of the house," said the Tabby.

"Good day to you, Tabby," said the man. "Have you had any food today?" he said.

"Oh, I've had a little, but I'm almost fasting," said the Tabby. "I've only had a bowl of porridge and a trough of drippings, and hey-hey if I don't take you too!" And then she went and gobbled the man up.

When she had done that, she went into the cowshed; there sat the old woman milking. "Good day to you, old woman in the cowshed," said the Tabby.

"Good day, is that you, Tabby?" said the old woman. "Have you eaten up your food?" she said.

"Oh, I've eaten a little today, but I'm almost fasting," said the Tabby. "I've only had a bowl of porridge, and a trough of drippings, and the man of the house, and hey-hey if I don't take you too!" she said, and then she went and gobbled up the old woman.

"Good day to you, cow in the stall," said the Tabby to the bell-cow.

Drawings by Th. Kittelsen

"Good day to you, Tabby," said the bell-cow. "Have you had any food today?" she said.

"Oh, I've had a little, but I'm almost fasting," said the Tabby. "I've only had a bowl of porridge, and a trough of drippings, and the man of the house, and the old woman in the cowshed, and hey-hey if I don't take you too!" said the Tabby, and then she went and gobbled up the bell-cow too.

Then she headed for the home pasture. There stood a man chopping leafy branches for fodder.

"Good day to you, fellow in the leafy woods," said the Tabby.

"Good day to you, Tabby; have you had any food today?" said the branch-chopper.

"Oh, I've had a little, but I'm almost fasting," said the Tabby. "I've only had a bowl of porridge, and a trough of drippings, and the man of the house, and the old woman in the cowshed, and the bell-cow in the stall, and hey-hey if I don't take you too!" she said, and then she went and gobbled up the branch-chopper too.

Then she came to a rock-pile. There stood the stoat, peeping out. "Good day to you, stoat in the rock-pile," said the Tabby.

"Good day to you, Tabby; have you had any food today?" said the stoat.

"Oh, I've had a little, but I'm almost fasting," said the Tabby. "I've only had a bowl of porridge, and a trough of drippings, and the man of the house, and the old woman in the cowshed, and the bell-cow in the stall, and the branch-chopper in the home pasture, and hey-hey if I don't take you too!" said the Tabby, and then she went and gobbled up the stoat too.

When she had gone a little farther, she came to a hazel bush. There sat the squirrel gathering nuts.

"Good day to you, squirrel in the bush," said the Tabby.

"Good day to you, Tabby; have you had any food today?" said the squirrel.

"Oh, I've had a little, but I'm almost fasting today," said the Tabby. "I've only had a bowl of porridge, and a trough of drippings, and the man of the house, and the old woman in the cowshed, and the bell-cow in the stall, and the branch-chopper in the home pasture, and the stoat in the rock-pile, and hey-hey if I don't take you too!" said the Tabby, and then she went and gobbled up the squirrel too.

When she had gone a bit farther she met the fox, who was slinking about on the edge of the woods.

"Good day to you, Slypaws," said the Tabby.

"Good day to you, Tabby; have you had any food today?" said the fox.

"Oh, I've had a little, but I'm almost fasting," said the Tabby. "I've only had a bowl of porridge, and a trough of drippings, and the man of the house, and the old woman in the cowshed, and the bell-cow in the stall, and the branch-chopper in the home pasture, and the stoat in the rock-pile, and the squirrel in the bush, and hey-hey if I don't take you too!" said the Tabby, and then she went and gobbled up the fox too.

When she had gone a little farther, she met a hare.

Then the Tabby went far, and farther than far.

"Good day to you, Hoppity Hare," said the Tabby.

"Good day to you, Tabby; have you had any food today?" said the hare.

"Oh, I've had a little, but I'm almost fasting," said the Tabby. "I've only had a bowl of porridge, and a trough of drippings, and the man of the house, and the old woman in the cowshed, and the bell-cow in the stall, and the branch-chopper in the home pasture and the stoat in the rock-pile, and the squirrel in the bush, and Slypaws the Fox, and hey-hey if I don't take you too!" said the Tabby, and then she went and gobbled up the hare too.

When she had gone a bit farther she met a wolf.

"Good day to you, Glutton Greylegs," said the Tabby.

"Good day to you, Tabby, have you had any food today?" said the wolf.

"Oh, I've had a little, but I'm almost fasting," said the Tabby. "I've only had a bowl of porridge, and a trough of drippings, and the man of the house, and the old woman in the cowshed, and the bell-cow in the stall, and the branch-chopper in the home pasture, and the stoat in the rock-pile, and the squirrel in the bush, and Slypaws the Fox, and Hoppity Hare, and hey-hey if I don't take you too!" said the Tabby, and then she went and gobbled up the wolf too.

Then she went to the forest, and when she had gone far, and farther than far, over hill and deep dale, she met a bear-cub.

"Good day to you, Frisky Bear," said the Tabby.

"Good day to you, Tabby; have you had any food today?" said the bear-cub.

"Oh, I've had a little, but I'm almost fasting," said the Tabby. "I've only had a bowl of porridge, and a trough of drippings, and the man of the house, and the old woman in the cowshed, and the bell-cow in the stall, and the branch-chopper in the home pasture, and the stoat in the rock-pile, and the squirrel in the bush, and Slypaws the Fox, and Hoppity Hare, and Glutton Greylegs, and hey-hey if I don't take you too!" said the Tabby, and then she went and gobbled up the bear-cub too.

When the Tabby had gone a bit farther, she met the she-bear who was clawing at the tree stumps until the splinters flew, so angry was she at losing her cub.

"Good day to you, Snappish She-bear," said the Tabby.

"Good day to you, Tabby; have you had any food today?" said the she-bear.

"Oh, I've had a little, but I'm almost fasting," said the Tabby. "I've only had a bowl of porridge, and a trough of drippings, and the man of the house, and the old woman in the cowshed, and the bell-cow in the stall, and the branch-chopper in the home pasture, and the stoat in the rock-pile and the squirrel in the bush, and Slypaws the Fox, and Hoppity Hare, and Glutton Greylegs, and Frisky Bear, and hey-hey if I don't take you too!" said the Tabby, and then she went and gobbled up the she-bear too.

When the Tabby had gone a little farther, she met the he-bear himself.

"Good day to you, Bruin Fine-Fellow," said the Tabby.

"Good day to you, Tabby; have you had any food today?" said the bear.

"Oh, I've had a little, but I'm almost fasting," said the Tabby. "I've only had

164

a bowl of porridge, and a trough of drippings, and the man of the house, and the old woman in the cowshed, and the bell-cow in the stall, and the branch-chopper in the home pasture, and the stoat in the rock-pile, and the squirrel in the bush, and Slypaws the Fox, and Hoppity Hare, and Glutton Greylegs, and Frisky Bear, and Snappish She-bear, and hey-hey if I don't take you too!" said the Tabby, and then she went and gobbled up the he-bear too.

Then the Tabby went far, and farther than far, until she came to a settled neighborhood again; there she met a bridal procession on the road.

"Good day to you, bridal procession on the road," said the Tabby.

"Good day to you, Tabby; have you had any food today?" said the bridal procession.

"Oh, I've had a little, but I'm almost fasting," said the Tabby. "I've only had a bowl of porridge, and a trough of drippings, and the man of the house, and the old woman in the cowshed, and the bell-cow in the stall, and the branch-chopper in the home pasture, and the stoat in the rock-pile, and the squirrel in the bush, and Slypaws the Fox, and Hoppity Hare, and Glutton Greylegs, and Frisky Bear, and Snappish She-bear, and Bruin Fine-Fellow, and hey-hey if I don't take you too!" said the Tabby, and then she flew at them, and gobbled up both bride and bridegroom, and the whole procession, with master of revels, and fiddler, and horses, and every last one of them.

When she had gone a bit farther, she came to the church. There she met a funeral procession.

"Good day to you, funeral procession by the church," said the Tabby.

"Good day to you, Tabby; have you had any food today?" said the funeral procession.

"Oh, I've had a little, but I'm almost fasting," said the Tabby. "I've only had a bowl of porridge, and a trough of drippings, and the man of the house, and the old woman in the cowshed, and the bell-cow in the stall, and the branch-chopper in the home pasture, and the stoat in the rock-pile, and the squirrel in the bush, and Slypaws the Fox, and Hoppity Hare, and Glutton Greylegs, and Frisky Bear, and Snappish She-bear, and Bruin Fine-Fellow, and the bridal procession on the road, and hey-hey if I don't take you too!" said the Tabby, and then she turned on the funeral procession and gobbled them up, mourners and all.

When the Tabby had put an end to them, she made her way up to the heavens, and when she had gone far, and farther than far, she met the Moon in the sky.

"Good day to you, Moon in the sky," said the Tabby.

"Good day to you, Tabby; have you had any food today?" said the Moon.

"Oh, I've had a little, but I'm almost fasting," said the Tabby. "I've only had a bowl of porridge, and a trough of drippings, and the man of the house, and the old woman in the cowshed, and the bell-cow in the stall, and the branch-chopper in the home pasture, and the stoat in the rock-pile, and the squirrel in the bush, and Slypaws the Fox, and Hoppity Hare, and Glutton Greylegs, and Frisky Bear, and Snappish She-bear, and Bruin Fine-Fellow, and the

165

bridal procession on the road, and the funeral procession by the church, and hey-hey if I don't take you too!" said the Tabby, and then she turned on the Moon and gobbled her up, both wax and wane.

Then the Tabby went far, and farther than far, until she met the Sun.

"Good day to you, Sun in the heavens," said the Tabby.

"Good day to you, Tabby; have you had any food today?" said the Sun.

"Oh, I've had a little," said the Tabby. "I've only had a bowl of porridge, and a trough of drippings, and the man of the house, and the old woman in the cowshed, and the bell-cow in the stall, and the branch-chopper in the home pasture, and the stoat in the rock-pile, and the squirrel in the bush, and Slypaws the Fox, and Hoppity Hare, and Glutton Greylegs, and Frisky Bear, and Snappish She-bear, and Bruin Fine-Fellow, and the bridal procession on the road, and the funeral procession by the church, and the Moon in the sky, and hey-hey if I don't take you too!" said the Tabby, and then she turned on the Sun in the heavens and gobbled him up.

Then the Tabby went far, and farther than far, until she came to a bridge. There she met a great big Billy-goat.

"Good day to you, Billy on the bridge so broad," said the Tabby.

"Good day to you, Tabby; have you had any food today?" said the Billy-goat.

"Oh, I've had a little, but I'm almost fasting," said the Tabby. "I've only had a bowl of porridge, and a trough of drippings, and the man of the house, and the old woman in the cowshed, and the bell-cow in the stall, and the branch-chopper in the home pasture, and the stoat in the rock-pile, and the squirrel in the bush, and Slypaws the Fox, and Hoppity Hare, and Glutton Greylegs,

and Frisky Bear, and Snappish She-bear, and Bruin Fine-Fellow, and the bridal procession on the road, and the funeral procession by the church, and the Moon in the sky, and the Sun in the heavens, and hey-hey if I don't take you too!" said the Tabby.

"You'll have to fight me first!" said the Billy-goat, and butted the Tabby so hard that she flew off the bridge and into the river, and there she burst.

Then out they crept, and home they flew, and were just as good as before, everyone the Tabby had eaten: the man of the house, and the old woman in the cowshed, and the bell-cow in the stall, and the branch-chopper in the home pasture, and the stoat in the rock-pile, and the squirrel in the bush, and Slypaws the Fox, and Hoppity Hare, and Glutton Greylegs, and Frisky Bear, and Snappish She-bear, and Bruin Fine-Fellow, and the bridal procession on the road, and the funeral procession by the church, and the Moon in the sky, and the Sun in the heavens.

THE DEVIL AND THE BAILIFF

There was once a bailiff who was a fleecer of the worst sort. One day the Devil came to fetch him.

"Never do I hear people say anything," he said, "but, 'Devil take that bailiff!' So now you'll have to come along with me. And, indeed, so bad are you that I don't believe you could be any wickeder or worse if you tried!"

"Well, if you *will* pay attention to all the things folk chatter about, then you have more to fly after than you can manage!" said the bailiff. "But, if you're such a kind man that you do everything folk ask you to, then *I* ought to be let off this time, too!" he said.

Indeed, the bailiff spoke up well for himself, and as the Devil was rather good-natured, they agreed at last to join company for a while. And the first person they met who bade the Devil take someone, *him* the Devil should take, and the bailiff should be set free.

"But it must come from the heart!" said the Devil.

First they came to a cottage. There stood the old woman churning butter, but when she saw strangers, she had to have a peek at them. In the meantime, along came her little pet pig, rooting and snuffing in every corner, and stuck its snout in the churn. Over it went, and the pig started gobbling up the cream.

"Was there ever a worse plague than a pig like that?" screamed the old woman. "Devil take you!" she said.

"Well, take the pig then!" said the bailiff.

"Do you think she's making me a present of the pork?" asked the Devil. "What would she have for her Sunday dinners in winter? No, that didn't come from the heart!"

So they walked on until they came to another cottage. Here the little child had been up to some mischief. "Right now I've had enough of you!" said the mother. "I do nothing else but wash and wipe and tidy up after this nasty brat! Devil take you!" she said.

Drawing by Th. Kittelsen.

"Well, take the child then!" said the bailiff.

"Oh, it doesn't come from the heart when a mother curses her child," said the Devil.

So they walked a bit farther. Then they met two farmers.

"There's that bailiff of ours," said one.

"Devil take that farmer-fleecer alive!" said the other.

"*That* came from the heart, it did!" said the Devil. "So come with me!"

And that time neither praying nor pleading helped.

THE ASH LAD AND THE GOOD HELPERS

There was once a king, and that king had heard tell of a ship that went just as fast on land as on water. So he too wanted to have such a ship, and to the one who could build it he promised his daughter and half the kingdom. And this he had proclaimed in all the churches throughout the land. There were many who tried, you might know, for surely half the kingdom would be good to have, they thought, and the king's daughter would be fine to have in the bargain. But all of them fared badly.

Now there were three brothers living in a parish away in the woods; the eldest was called Per, the next one Paul, and the youngest was called Espen Ash Lad, because he always sat, and poked and raked in the ashes. But on the Sunday when the proclamation was made about the ship the king wanted, it just happened that he was at church — he too. When he came home and told the others about it, Per, who was the eldest, asked his mother for provisions, for now he wanted to set out and see if he couldn't build the ship, and win the king's daughter and half the kingdom.

When he had got the knapsack of provisions on his back, he strode off. On the way he met a bent and wizzened old man.

"Where are you off to?" said the man.

"I'm going off to the woods to make a trough for my father. He doesn't like to eat with the rest of us," said Per.

"Trough it'll be!" said the man. "What've you got in your knapsack?"

Drawings by Th. Kittelsen.

170

The ship that went just as well on land as on water.

"Manure!" said Per.

"Manure it'll be!" said the man.

So Per strode over to the oak grove and chopped and built for all he was worth; but for all he chopped, and for all he built, all he turned out was troughs and more troughs. When it was getting on to lunch time, and he was going to have something to eat, he opened the knapsack. But it wasn't food that was in the sack. And as he now had nothing to eat, and he fared no better with the building, he got tired of the work, put the axe and the knapsack on his back, and went off home to his mother again.

Then Paul wanted to set out, and try his hand at building the ship and winning the king's daughter and half the kingdom. He asked his mother for provisions, and when he had got them, he put the knapsack on his back and set out for the woods. On the way he met a bent and wizened old man.

"Where are you off to?" said the man.

"Oh, I'm going off to the woods to make a pig-trough for that little piglet of ours," said Paul.

"Pig-trough it'll be!" said the man. "What have you got in your sack?" asked the man.

"Manure!" said Paul.

"Manure it'll be!" said the man.

So Paul strode off to the woods, and started chopping and building for all he was worth. But no matter how he chopped, and no matter how he put the wood together, he turned out nothing but trough-shapes and pig-troughs. He didn't give up, though, but kept at it until late in the afternoon before he thought of having a little to eat. Then he was so hungry, all at once, that he had to get out his knapsack. But when he took it up, there wasn't a crumb of food in it. Paul was so angry that he wrung the sack inside out and dashed it against a stump, and took the axe and strode out of the woods, and made for home straightaway.

When Paul had come home, the Ash Lad wanted to set out, and asked his mother for provisions. "Maybe I could manage to get the ship built, and win the king's daughter and half the kingdom," he said.

"Yes, that'd be likely!" said his mother. "You, who never do anything but root and rake in the ashes! No! You'll get no provisions!" said the old woman.

The Ash Lad didn't give up for that. He pleaded so long that at last he was allowed to go. He got no provisions, not likely! But he sneaked along a couple of oatcakes and a drop of stale beer, and set out on his way.

When he had gone a short distance, he met the same bent and wizzened old fellow, who was so feeble.

"Where are you off to?" said the man.

"Oh, I was going to the woods, as it happens, to build a ship which goes just as well on land as on water," said the Ash Lad. "For the king has proclaimed that the one who can build such a ship will get the king's daughter and half the kingdom," he said.

"What do you have in your sack?" asked the man.

"Oh, it's not much to speak of. It's meant to be provisions," replied the Ash Lad.

"If you'll give me a little of your provisions, I shall help you," said the man.

"Gladly," said the Ash Lad, "but it's nothing more than a couple of oatcakes and a drop of stale beer."

It did not matter to the old man what it was; if only he got it, he would help him all right.

When they came to the old oak in the woods, the man said, "Now you're to cut out a chip and put it in again where it came from. And, when you've done that, you can lie down and go to sleep."

Well, the Ash Lad did as the old man said: he lay down to sleep, and in his sleep it seemed to him that he heard chopping, and hammering, and building, and sawing, and joining; but he could not wake up before the man woke him. There stood the ship, completely finished, alongside the oak.

"Now you're to climb aboard, and you're to take everyone you meet with you," said the fellow. Well, Espen Ash Lad thanked him for the ship, and sailed away, and said he would do as the man told him.

When he had sailed a little way, he came to a long, skinny knave who lay on a hillside eating rubble.

"What sort of a fellow are you to be lying here eating rubble?" asked the Ash Lad.

The knave said he was so hungry for meat that he could never got his fill. That was why he had to eat rubble. And then he asked if he could come along on the ship.

"If you want to come along, just climb in," said the Ash Lad.

Yes, that he'd like of course, and so he took some rubble with him for provisions.

When they had sailed a bit farther, they met a fellow who was lying on a sunny hillside sucking a barrel tap.

... he came to a long, skinny knave who lay on a hillside eating rubble.

"What sort of a fellow are you?" said Espen Ash Lad. "And what's the good of lying sucking that barrel tap?"

"Oh, when one hasn't got the barrel, one must make do with the tap," said the man. "I'm always so thirsty that I can never drink my fill of beer or wine," he said, and then he asked if he could come along on the ship.

"If you want to come along, just climb in," said the Ash Lad.

Yes, that he'd like, so he climbed aboard, and took the tap with him for the sake of his thirst.

When they had sailed a bit farther, they met a man who was lying with one ear to the ground, listening.

"What sort of fellow are you, and what's the good of lying on the ground listening?" said Espen Ash Lad.

"I'm listening to the grass, for my hearing is so good that I can hear it grow," he said, and then he asked if he could come along on the ship.

There was no refusing him. "If you want to come along, just climb in," said the Ash Lad.

Yes, that he'd like, and so he climbed aboard — he too!

When they had sailed a bit farther, they came to a man who was standing and aiming a gun.

"What sort of fellow are you, and what's the good of standing and aiming like that?" said the Ash Lad.

"My sight is so keen," he said, "that without difficulty I can shoot straight to the world's end." Then he asked if he could come along on the ship.

"If you want to come along, just climb in," said the Ash Lad.

Yes, that he'd like, and climbed up.

When they had sailed a bit farther, they came to a man hopping about on one foot, and on the other he had seven hundred-weights.

"What sort of a fellow are you, and what's the good of hopping about on one foot, with seven hundred-weights on the other?"

"I'm so fleet-footed," he said, "that if I walked on both feet, I'd come to the end of the world in less than five minutes." Then he asked if he could come along on the ship.

"If you want to come along, just climb in," said the Ash Lad.

Yes, that he'd like, and so he climbed up in the ship to join the Ash Lad and his companions.

When they had sailed a bit farther, they met a man who stood holding his hand over his mouth.

"What sort of a fellow are you," said the Ash Lad, "and what's the good of standing like that and holding your hand over your mouth?" he said.

"Oh, I've got seven summers and fifteen winters inside my body!" he said. "So I'd better hold my mouth, for if I let them out all at once, they'd put an end to the world right away," he said, and then he asked if he could come along.

"If you want to come along, just climb in," said the Ash Lad.

Yes, he'd like to come along, so he climbed aboard the ship with the others.

174

When they had sailed a good while, they came to the king's manor.

The Ash Lad strode right in to the king and said that the ship was standing ready in the yard, and now he wanted the king's daughter, just as the king has promised.

The king wasn't any too pleased about this, for the Ash Lad didn't look as if he was worth very much. He was both black and sooty, and the king hardly wanted to give his daughter to such a tramp. So he said he'd have to wait a while. He couldn't have the princess before he had emptied a storehouse of the king's which had three hundred barrels of meat in it. "It's all the same — if you can get it done by this time tomorrow, you shall have her," said the king.

"I'll have to try," said the Ash Lad, "but I suppose I'll be allowed to take one of my comrades along, won't I?"

Yes, he could do that — he could even take all six with him, said the king, for he thought the task was out-and-out impossible.

The Ash Lad only took with him the man who ate rubble, and was always so hungry for meat. And no sooner had they unlocked the storehouse, than he had eaten it all up, so there was nothing left but six small shoulders of salt mutton, one for each of the others on board.

Then the Ash Lad strode in to the king and told him that the storehouse was empty, and now he must surely get the king's daughter.

The king went out to the storehouse, and found it empty right enough. But the Ash Lad was still black and sooty, and the king thought it was really too bad that such a tramp should wed his daughter. So he said he had a cellar full of beer and old wine — three hundred barrels of each — which he wanted to have drunk up first. "And it's a sure thing, if you're man enough to drink them up by this time tomorrow, then you shall have her," said the king.

"I'll have to try," said the Ash Lad. "But I suppose I'll be allowed take one of my comrades along, won't I?"

"Yes, certainly," said the king. He felt he had so much beer and wine that they would be well taken care of — all seven!

The Ash Lad took with him the man who sucked the tap, and always thirsted after beer; and then the king locked them down in the cellar. There the man drank barrel after barrel, as long as there was anything left. But in the last one he left a drop, so there would be a couple of tankards apiece for each of his comrades.

In the morning the cellar was unlocked, and straightaway the Ash Lad strode in to the king and said he had dealt with the beer and wine, and now he surely must get the king's daughter, just as he had been promised.

"Well, first I must go down to the cellar and see," said the king, for he didn't believe it. When he came down to the cellar, there were nothing but empty barrels. But the Ash Lad was still black and sooty, and the king felt it was unseemly to have such a son-in-law. Just the same, he said, if the boy could fetch water from the world's end for the princess's tea in ten minutes,

175

then he should get both her and half the kingdom! For *that* was out-and-out impossible, he believed.

"I'll have to try," said the Ash Lad.

So he got hold of the one who hopped on one foot and had seven hundred-weights on the other, and said he must kick off the weights and use both legs as fast as he could, for he had to have water from the world's end for the princess's tea in ten minutes!

The man took off the weights, got a pail, and set out — and gone he was in a flash. But time dragged on and on — seven long and seven broad — and he didn't come back.

He took off the weights, got a pail, and set out — and gone he was in a flash.

At last there were only three minutes before the time was up, and the king was as delighted as if he had been given a shilling.

But then the Ash Lad shouted to the man who could hear the grass grow, and told him to listen to find out what had become of the other.

"He has fallen asleep beside the well," he said. "I can hear him snoring, and the Troll is combing his hair."

So the Ash Lad shouted to the one who could shoot straight to the world's end, and bade him put a shot into the Troll. Yes, this he did! He shot him right in the eye. The Troll let out a roar, so that the man who was to fetch the tea-water woke up at once. And when he came to the king's manor, there was still a minute of the ten left.

The Ash Lad strode in to the king and said that here was the water, and now he surely must get the king's daughter, there was certainly no more to be said about that. But the king thought that he was as black and sooty as ever, and he didn't like having him for a son-in-law. So the king said that he had three hundred cords of wood with which he was going to dry the grain in the bathhouse," and it's all the same, if you're man enough to sit in there and burn it up, then you shall have her. There's nothing more to be said about that," he said.

"I'll have to try," said the Ash Lad, "but I suppose I can take one of my comrades along with me, can't I?"

"Yes, all six if you like," said the king, for he thought it would be hot enough for them all.

The Ash Lad took with him the man who had the fifteen winters and seven summers in his body, and strode into the bathhouse in the evening. But the king had got such a roaring fire going, that they could easily have cast stoves of iron. They could not get out, for no sooner were they in than the king barred the door and put on a couple of extra padlocks.

So the Ash Lad said; "You'll have to let out six or seven winters so there'll be a passable summer warmth."

Then they managed to hold out in there, but as night was drawing on, it became quite chilly. So the Ash Lad told him to warm it up a bit with a couple of summers, and then they slept until well into the next day. But when they heard the king rummaging about outside, the Ash Lad said, "Now you must let out a couple more winters, but do it so that the last one goes right in his face!"

Yes, he did just that, and when the king opened up the bathhouse, thinking they were lying there burnt to a cinder, they sat shivering and freezing so their teeth were chattering, and the man with the fifteen winters in his body let go the last one right in the king's face, so a big chilblain appeared.

"*Do I get the king's daughter now?*" said the Ash Lad.

"Yes! Take her and keep her, and take the kingdom too!" said the king. He dared not say 'No' any longer.

So they held the wedding, and reveled and made merry, and fired off shots to scare away troll hags! And, as they were rushing about groping for a bullet wadding, they mistook me for one, and gave me porridge in a flask and milk in a basket, and shot me straight here so I could tell you how it all came about.

GUDBRAND OF THE HILLSIDE

Once upon a time there was a man whose name was Gudbrand; he had a farm which lay far up on a hillside, and so they called him 'Gudbrand of the Hillside'. He and his wife lived so happily together, and were on such good terms, that whatever the husband did, the wife thought it so well done that it could never be done better. No matter how he went about anything, she was just as happy. They owned their farm, and had a hundred *dalers* laid up at the bottom of the chest, and two cows tethered in the barn.

But one day the wife said, "I think we should go to town with one of the cows and sell her, then we could have some pocket money. We're such fine folk that we can just as well have some ready cash as other people do. We can't dip into the hundred dalers lying at the bottom of the chest, but I don't know what we need with more than one cow. And we'd gain a little by it too, in that I'd get off with caring for one instead of feeding and cleaning up after two."

Well, Gudbrand thought this was both well and rightly said, so he took the cow and went to town to sell it. But when he came to the town, there was no one who wanted to buy his cow. "Well, well," thought Gudbrand, "I can just go home again with the cow. I know I have both stall and tether for her, and the road back is no longer than the road here." And with that he started dawdling home again.

But when he had gone a mile or two on the way, he met a man who had a horse he wanted to sell, and as Gudbrand thought it would be better to have a horse than a cow, he traded with the man. When he had gone a little farther, he met a man driving a fat pig before him, and now Gudbrand thought it

Drawings by Th. Kittelsen

would be better to have a fat pig than a horse, so he traded with the man. He went a little farther, and then he met a man with a goat. Gudbrand thought very likely it would be better to have a goat than a pig, so he traded with the man. Then he walked a long way until he met a man who had a sheep, and he traded with him too, for he thought: "It's always better to have a sheep than a goat." Now when he had gone another short distance he met a man who had a goose, so he swapped his sheep for the goose. And after he had gone a long way farther, he met a man with a rooster. Again he traded with the man, for he thought this way: "It's always better to have a rooster than a goose."

He walked on until it was late in the day, and he began to be hungry. So he sold the rooster for twelve shillings, and bought himself something to eat with the money. "It's better to save a life than to have a rooster," thought Gudbrand of the Hillside. Then he continued on his way home until he came to the farm of his nearest neighbor. There he went in.

"Well, how did you make out in town today?" asked the people.

"Oh, so-so," said Gudbrand of the Hillside. "I can't exactly brag about my luck, but neither can I complain about it." And with that he told his story from beginning to end.

"Well, you *will* have a hot reception when you get home to your wife," said the farmer. "Heaven help you! I wouldn't want to be in your place."

"I think it could have turned out worse," said Gudbrand of the Hillside. "But whether it's turned out well or badly, my old woman is so kind-hearted that she never says anything, no matter what I do."

"Well, to be sure that's what I hear, not that I believe it," said the neighbor.

"Are you willing to make a bet with me about it?" asked Gudbrand of the Hillside. "I have a hundred dalers stored away at the bottom of the chest at home. Do you dare to put up an equal amount as a bet?"

Well, they made the bet, and then Gudbrand stayed at his neighbor's until evening. After dark they pottered off together to Gudbrand's farm. There the neighbor stayed outside the door to listen, while Gudbrand went inside by himself to his old woman.

"Good evening," said Gudbrand of the Hillside when he came in.

"Good evening," said the wife. "Oh, God be praised! Is that you?"

Yes, that it was.

Then the wife asked how he had made out in town.

"Oh, so-so," answered Gudbrand. "Not much to brag about. When I got to town there was no one who wanted to buy the cow, so I swapped it for a horse, I did."

"Well, you shall really have thanks for that," said the wife. "We're good enough people to drive to church like other folks. And as long as we can afford to have a horse, we may just as well get used to one. Go down and let in the horse, children!"

"Well," said Gudbrand, "I don't have the horse any more. When I had gone a bit on the way I swapped it for a pig."

179

"And thanks to you for that!" said the wife.

"Nay! Nay!" cried the wife. "That's just what I would have done! You deserve a thousand thanks. Now we can have pork in the house, and something to set before people when they look in on us, we too! What would we need a horse for? People would only say we had become so high and mighty that we could no longer *walk* to church as before. Go down and let in the pig, children!"

180

"But I don't have the pig, either," said Gudbrand. "When I came a bit farther, I swapped it for a goat."

"Oh nay! Oh nay! How well you do everything!" cried the wife. "When I really think of it, what should I do with a pig? People would only have said, 'over there they eat up everything they have'. Nay, with a goat I'll get both milk and cheese, and still keep the goat. Let in the goat, children!"

"But I haven't got the goat anymore, either," said Gudbrand. "When I came a bit farther, I swapped the goat and got a strapping sheep instead."

"Nay!" cried the wife. "You've done everything exactly as I should have wished; exactly as if I should have been along myself. What should we do with a goat? I would have had to scramble up and down hill and dale, and get it down again in the evening. No, if I have a sheep, I can get wool and clothing in the house, and food, too. Go down and let in the sheep, children!"

"But now I haven't got the sheep any longer," said Gudbrand, "for when I had gone on a bit, I swapped it for a goose!"

"And thanks to you for that!" said the wife. "And many thanks too! What should I do with a sheep? Why, I have neither spinning wheel nor spindle, nor do I care about toiling, and cutting, and making clothes, either. We can buy clothes now as before. Now I'll have a roast goose, which I've been wanting for such a long time, and I can have down for my little pillow. Go down and let in the goose, children!"

"But now I have no goose, either," said Gudbrand. "When I had come a bit farther on the way, I swapped it for a rooster."

"I don't know how you've hit upon everything," cried the wife. "It's all just as I would have done it myself. A rooster! That's the same as if you had bought an eight-day clock. For every morning the rooster crows at four o'clock, so we can get up at the right time, too. What, indeed, should we do with the goose? I don't know how to roast it, and my pillow I can fill with grass. Go out and let in the rooster, children!"

"But I don't have the rooster, either," said Gudbrand. "When I had gone still farther, I became as hungry as a wolf, and so I had to sell the rooster for twelve shillings to save my life."

"Nay! Praise God that you did!" cried the wife. "How you do take care of yourself. You do everything just as I could have wished. What should we do with the rooster? Why, we are our own masters, we can lie in bed in the morning as long as we wish, thank heaven. As long as I have you back again, who manages everything so well, I need neither rooster nor goose, neither pig nor cow."

Then Gudbrand opened the door.

"Have I won those hundred *dalers* now?" he said, and the neighbor had to admit that he had.

THE TWELVE WILD DUCKS

Once upon a time there was a queen who went out driving. It was winter and the snow was fresh on the ground. When she had gone only a little way, her nose started to bleed, and she had to get out of the sleigh. As she stood up by the fence and looked at the red blood on the white snow, she came to think that she had twelve sons and no daughter, and so she said to herself, "If I had a daughter as white as snow and as red as blood, it wouldn't matter at all about my sons."

She had scarcely uttered these words, when a Troll-hag stood before her and said, "You shall have a daughter, and she shall be as white as snow and as red as blood, and then your sons shall belong to me. But you may keep them with you until the child has been christened."

When the time came, the queen gave birth to a daughter, and she was as white as snow and as red as blood, just as the Troll-hag had promised, and so they called her 'Snow-White-Rose-Red'. There was great rejoicing at the king's court, and the queen was so happy that there was no limit to it. But when she remembered what she had promised the Troll-hag, she had a silversmith make twelve silver spoons, one for each prince, and then she had him make one more, and she gave it to Snow-White-Rose-Red.

As soon as the princess had been christened, the princes were transformed into twelve wild ducks and flew their way, and they were never seen again; gone they were and gone they stayed. The princess grew up, and became both

Drawings by Th. Kittelsen

182

tall and beautiful, but she was often so strange and sad that no one could understand what was the matter with her.

One evening the queen, too, was sad, for she must have had many strange thoughts when she remembered her sons, and so she asked Snow-White-Rose-Red, "Why are you so sad, my child? If there is anything wrong, then say so! If there is anything you wish, you shall have it!"

"Oh, I find it so lonely here," said Snow-White-Rose-Red. "Everyone else has brothers and sisters, but I am so alone, I have none. That is why I am so sad."

"You, too, have brothers, my child. I had twelve sons who were your brothers, but I gave them away to have you." And then the queen told her the whole story.

When the princess heard that, she had no more peace of mind; and no matter how much the queen cried and carried on, it was no use. She wanted to go away, as she felt that she was to blame for everything; and at last she left the king's palace. She walked and she walked — so far out in the wide world that you wouldn't believe so fine a maiden could walk so far.

One day, when she had been walking a long time in a deep, deep forest, she got tired and sat down on a mound, and there she fell asleep. Then she dreamed that she walked farther into the forest until she came to a small log cabin, and there she found her brothers. All at once she woke up, and right in front of her she saw a well-trodden path in the green moss, and that path led deeper into the forest. She followed it, and after a long walk she came to a little log cabin exactly like the one she had seen in her dream. When she went inside, there was nobody there, but there stood twelve beds, and twelve chairs and twelve spoons, and there were twelve of everything else in the cabin. When she saw this, she became happier than she had been for many a year, for she knew at once that her brothers lived there, and they were the ones who owned the beds, and the chairs and the spoons. And right away she made a fire, swept the floor, made the beds, and tidied up as best she could; and when she had cooked a meal for them all, she sat down to eat. But she forgot her spoon on the table. Then she crept under the youngest brother's bed and lay down there.

She had lain there only a moment, when she heard a whistling and a whirring in the air, and the next instant all the twelve ducks came rushing in; but as soon as they crossed the threshold they turned into princes.

"Oh, how nice and warm it is in here," they said. "God bless whoever has made the fire and cooked such good food for us!" And each one took his silver spoon and was going to eat.

But when each one had taken his own, there was still a spoon on the table, and it was so like the others that they could not tell it apart from them. They looked at each other in bewilderment.

"That is our sister's spoon," they said, "and if the spoon is here, she cannot be so far away either."

"If that is our sister's spoon, and she is to be found here, she shall be killed, for she is the cause of all our misery," said the eldest brother. All this the sister heard where she was hiding under the bed.

183

There was a whistling and a whirring in the air, and then twelve wild ducks came flying.

"No," said the youngest of the princes, "it would be a sin to kill her for that; it is not her fault that we suffer. If anyone is to blame, it must be our own mother."

They started searching, both high and low, and at last they looked under all the beds, too; and when they came to the bed of the youngest prince, they found her and dragged her out.

The eldest prince still wanted her to be killed, but she cried and pleaded so pitiably, "Oh, please, please don't kill me. I have been wandering for many years trying to find you, and if I could only save you, I would gladly give my own life."

"Well, if you will free us," they said, "you shall live; for if you want to, then you can well enough."

"Yes, just tell me how it can be done, and I will do it, whatever it may be," said the princess.

"You must gather thistledown," said the princes, "and *that* you must card, and spin, and weave into cloth. And when you have done that, you must cut and sew twelve caps, twelve shirts, and twelve scarves, one for each of us. And while you are doing that, you must neither speak, nor laugh, nor cry. If you can do it, we are freed."

"But where will I find thistledown enough for so many scarves and caps and shirts?" said Snow-White-Rose-Red.

"We will show you, all right," they said, and led her down to a large bog which was so full of thistledown waving in the wind and glittering in the sun that it shone like snow a long way off.

Never had the princess seen so much thistledown before, and right away she started picking and gathering, as well and fast as she was able; and when she came home in the evening, she began to card and spin it into yarn. She kept at it for a long time; she gathered thistledown, and carded, and in between she cared for the princes, cooked their meals and made their beds.

At dusk they returned home, rushing and roaring like wild ducks. During the night they were princes, but in the morning they flew away again, and were wild ducks the whole day.

But then it happened that once when she was at the bog picking thistledown (and, if I'm not mistaken, it was the last time she was to go there) the young king who ruled the country was out hunting, and came riding over to the bog and caught sight of her. He stopped, and wondered who this lovely maiden could be, wandering about in the bog collecting thistledown, and he asked her, too. And when he got no answer to his question, he wondered even more, and he thought so well of her that he wanted to take her home with him to the castle and marry her. So he told his servants to lift her up on his horse. Snow-White-Rose-Red wrung her hands and made signs to them and pointed to the sacks she had worked so hard to fill with thistledown. When the king understood that she wanted to take them along, he told the servants to load the sacks, too. When they had done that, the princess calmed down, for the king was as kind as he was handsome, and he was gentle and friendly towards her.

Never had the princess seen so much thistledown before.

But when they came home to the king's castle, and the old queen, who was his stepmother, caught sight of Snow-White-Rose-Red, she was so angry and envious, because the princess was so pretty, that she said to the king, "Don't you understand that this girl you have brought home and want to marry is a witch? She neither speaks, nor laughs, nor cries."

The king paid no attention to what she said, but held a wedding and married Snow-White-Rose-Red, and they lived in great joy and splendor; but for all that, she never left off sewing the shirts.

Before a year had gone, Snow-White-Rose-Red gave birth to a little prince, and that made the old queen even more angry and envious. And when it was getting on toward night, she stole into Snow-White-Rose-Red's room while she slept, took the child, and threw it into the snake-pit. Then she cut the queen's finger and smeared the blood on her mouth, and then went to the king.

"Now come and see," she said, "what sort of a queen you have married. She has eaten up her own child."

At this the king was so upset that he almost wept, and he said, "Yes, it must indeed be true, since I can see it with my own eyes. But I am sure she will never do it again. So I will spare her life this time."

Before the next year was over, she gave birth to another son, and with him it went just as with the first. The king's stepmother became even more angry and jealous, so she stole into the queen's room during the night while she slept, took the child and threw it into the snake-pit, cut the queen's finger, and smeared the blood on her mouth; and told the king that the queen had eaten up this child, too. Then the king was so distressed that you never saw the like, and so he said, "Yes, it must indeed be true, since I see it with my own eyes, but I am sure she will never do it again, so I will spare her this time, too."

Before another year had passed, Snow-White-Rose-Red gave birth to a daughter, and this child, too, the old queen threw down into the snake-pit. While the young queen was asleep, she cut her finger, smeared the blood on her mouth, and then went to the king and said, "Now you can come and see if it isn't just as I say, that she is a witch, for now she has eaten up her third child, too!"

This time the young king was so grief-stricken that he could not be comforted, for now he could spare her no longer, but had to give orders that she should be burned alive. When the pyre was ablaze, and she was about to be placed on it, she made signs to take twelve boards and stand them around the fire, and on them she hung the caps, and the shirts and the scarves for her brothers. But the shirt for her youngest brother had the left sleeve missing as she had not had time to get it finished. Hardly had she done this than they heard a whistling and whirring in the air, and then twelve wild ducks came flying over the tree tops, and each one took his clothing in his bill and flew away with it.

There lay the three children playing with snakes and toads.

"Now you can see," said the wicked queen to the king, "now you can really see that she is a witch. Hurry up and throw her into the fire before the logs burn up!"

"Never mind," said the young king. "We have logs enough, the whole forest is full of wood. I want to wait a while and see how this all turns out."

At this moment the twelve princes came riding, as handsome and well-built as anyone could wish to see; but the youngest prince had a duck's wing instead of his left arm.

"What is going on here?" asked the princes.

"My queen is to be burned because she is a witch, and has eaten up her own children," replied the king.

"She has not eaten her children," said the princes. "Speak now, sister. Now that you have freed us, save yourself!"

Then Snow-White-Rose-Red spoke, and told them all that had happened, that each time she had a child, the old queen, the king's stepmother, had sneaked into her room during the night, taken the baby from her, and cut her finger and smeared the blood on her mouth. And the princes took the king and led him to the snake-pit; there lay the three children playing with snakes and toads, and lovelier children you could never see in a lifetime.

The king took them back to his stepmother, and asked her what punishment

188

she thought fit for one who could have the heart to betray an innocent queen and three such lovely children?

"Anyone who did that should be tied to twelve wild horses and torn to bits," said the old queen.

"You have declared your own punishment," said the young king, "and such shall be your fate."

And so the wicked old queen was tied to twelve wild horses, and torn to bits.

But Snow-White-Rose-Red, the king, and their children, and the twelve princes, all rode back to her parents and told them what had happened. So there was great rejoicing throughout the whole kingdom, because the princess was freed and had freed her twelve brothers too.